SYDNEY J. BOUNDS

◆

THE OTHER CISCO KID

Complete and Unabridged

LINFORD
Leicester

First published in Great Britain in 2003
as
The Other Cisco Kid by Sam Foster

First Linford Edition
published 2016

A catalogue record for this book is available
from the British Library.

ISBN 978–1–4448–2822–1

Published by
F. A. Thorpe (Publishing)
Anstey, Leicestershire

Set by Words & Graphics Ltd.
Anstey, Leicestershire
Printed and bound in Great Britain by
T. J. International Ltd., Padstow, Cornwall

This book is printed on acid-free paper

THE OTHER CISCO KID

When young Billy Baxter takes up with the Cisco Kid, the outlaw has a surprising proposition for him. Having been offered a marshal position in two separate towns, the Kid suggests that he and Baxter fill both vacancies between them — with the youth assuming the Kid's identity, banking on the outlaw's reputation deterring would-be challengers. Eager for adventure, Baxter accepts, and takes up the star in Prospect. But he'll find that the town holds far more adventure than he'd bargained for . . .

1

Strange Partners

Young Billy Baxter, sitting beside the driver of a covered wagon, came down a deeply rutted track from the Rockies. He clung to the brake handle, shaking so his teeth rattled, as wagon wheels jolted a way down the mountainside towards the prairie.

The air was clear and the view of trees and grassland extensive and exhilarating; he would have been tempted to whistle a tune if he hadn't been afraid of biting his tongue clean off next time they dropped into a pothole.

The driver's expression was sour as spoiled milk. For him, returning from the San Francisco area was an admission of failure; the promise of easy gold had not materialized. The wagon Baxter

1

rode was the last of three making up the train going east and he was excited by the thought of setting out on an adventure. This was his first glimpse of a wild country he'd only read about.

A shot blasted his ears, echoing and making him jump. A voice called, 'Halt those horses, driver — brake, brake!'

Baxter was aware of the leading two wagons disappearing rapidly as they made a run for it, whips cracking.

A bullet passed between him and the driver and the horses panicked and tried to swerve. The wagon lurched sideways, a wheel stuck in a rut and it overturned.

Baxter was thrown from his seat and, for a moment, lay stunned. He heard the driver cursing, his voice muffled until he spat out a plug of half-chewed tobacco.

'Goddamn it to hell, you stupid bastard! We've got no gold — that's why we're going back.'

The hold-up man smiled. 'No? But I bet you're carrying supplies for a long journey, and I'm clean out of everything.'

Baxter sat up and tried out a few cuss-words himself. He jammed his hat back on his head and climbed to his feet. His denim pants and flannel shirt had acquired a layer of dirt so they no longer looked store-new. Still in a daze, his hand touched the butt of a Colt revolver holstered at his belt.

The hold-up man drawled, 'D'you figure on pulling that gun, youngster? D'you know who I am?'

Baxter's mouth tasted dry as dust and he let his hand fall away, empty. The hold-up man wore no mask and his face had hard lines beneath a Stetson.

'No, sir. I've seen your picture in the papers. You're the one they call the Cisco Kid.'

The driver freed his horses and started to throw supplies into a sack: bacon, beans, flour, salt, coffee and tobacco. 'Are you going to help get this wagon upright?' he asked.

The Kid's smile was frigid. 'Reckon to just mosey along. Could be your friends will turn back to help yuh.'

The driver snorted. 'That's likely, ain't it?'

The Kid gave Billy Baxter a long hard look, then nodded. 'Guess I'll take you along too, youngster. Throw a saddle on a horse and mount up.'

'Me?' Baxter was startled, then alarmed.

The wagon driver swore. 'Hell, you can't leave me a horse short!'

The Kid placed a bullet between his boots and he sprang back.

'Can't I?'

Baxter, scared now, dragged a saddle from the wagon and got it on to the quietest of the four horses.

'What d'yuh want him for?' the wagon driver asked suspiciously. 'He ain't nobody — just paid cash for a ride out west.'

The Kid smiled again, but gave no answer. 'Tighten those cinches,' he said. 'You lead off, downhill,' he ordered, and Baxter obeyed, feeling uncomfortable with an armed man at his back.

They rode on until the driver's curses faded, then the Cisco Kid said, 'Take the track leading between the trees.'

The track, made by wild animals, wound between shrubs that screened them from view, descending all the while towards the prairie. If he hadn't been feeling so nervous, Baxter could have enjoyed the ride.

'What do they call you?' the Kid asked.

'Billy.'

'Waal, Billy, you call me Kid. You remind me of myself when I was young. I figure you're looking for excitement, right?'

Baxter muttered, 'Yes,' and the Kid laughed.

'So now you're having an adventure. You can relax — I don't mean you any harm.'

The track meandered between trees and sometimes branches lashed Baxter's face.

'You're making too much noise,' the Kid said. 'You must learn to ride without disturbing anything.'

Further on, Baxter heard the trickle of running water and they came to an open space beside a clump of alders. The Kid dismounted. 'Make camp here.'

Baxter collected dry wood and the Kid got a small fire going, greased a tin pan and cut slices of bacon to cook. He boiled water for coffee.

Baxter forgot he was in a dangerous position when he suddenly found his appetite. He speared bacon with his sheath-knife, polished off beans and biscuits and helped himself to coffee. His dread of the outlaw diminished with each mouthful.

The Cisco Kid stretched out, his back against the trunk of a tree. He rolled a cigarette and lit up. The setting sun gave a warm glow, softening the angles of his face.

'You listening, Billy?'

'Sure.'

'In the morning I'm going to put a proposition to you, so don't try any stunts in the night. I sleep light and my gun's on a hair-trigger.'

The Kid chose a shadowy place, rolled himself in a blanket with his saddle for a headrest and was asleep in an instant.

Baxter found the uneven ground a hard mattress and the air chill after the sun went down. He found it difficult to sleep, his brain churning with questions. Why had the Kid picked him out? What was his proposition? He was in a fever of agitation, wary, but excited too.

He kept changing position, trying to get comfortable. Small animals made rustling noises and, from the undergrowth, something sneaked close, bright-eyed and sniffing.

This was very different from his life in San Francisco, working in a general store with the owner shouting at him to stop day-dreaming. That had been his routine, serving customers with coats, denim and boots; miners with picks and shovels; day after day the same, boring. The miners headed for the gold-fields while he dreamed of adventure, but it wasn't digging for gold he craved.

After work, in his room in the boarding-house where he lodged, he dug out the small library of dime novels he'd accumulated over time.

It was the excitement of the West that fired his imagination, the life of a Pony Express rider, a trail scout, or the cowboys he read about night after night by the flickering light of a candle.

He thrilled to tales of wild Bill, Indian fighter; Texas Jack's daring adventures on the track of outlaws; the heroes of *Wild West Weekly*; Hawkeye, the intrepid hunter, or the men of the Arizona Rangers . . . and now he would be a real Westerner, like them.

Baxter dozed off, still defending his scalp above the uniform of a cavalry soldier; and woke to the smell of boiling coffee. The Cisco Kid had a small fire burning and was slicing bacon into a pan.

'I guess a youngster needs his sleep,' he drawled, 'but this ain't a regular hotel. If you're going to partner me, you'll need to cultivate the knack of sleeping with one eye open. Or have you forgotten there's a price on my head?'

'Partner?' A thrill ran through him as Baxter struggled upright, hardly believing his ears. Partner the Cisco Kid?

He emptied his bladder against a tree and sloshed creek water over his face. The mountain air had already alerted his appetite and he ate hungrily.

The Kid seemed mildly amused. 'Guess you're even more the way I used to be than I'd realized.'

His mare walked up to him and he rubbed her nose and fondled her ears.

Baxter stared at the horse; to him she was ugly, all legs and teeth. 'A horse is a horse, I suppose, but — '

The Kid frowned. 'You've got that wrong, Billy. This one is special — she's got the stamina to keep going after the others have dropped behind. She's saved my life more than once.'

Baxter regarded the mare with new insight, impressed; she glared back with bared teeth and a wicked gleam in her eyes.

The Kid finished his breakfast and told Baxter to clean up the camp. He rolled a cigarette and smoked quietly till the chore was completed to his satisfaction.

'Never leave your campsite so it's obvious where you were — try not to leave a single trace. Now, listen. This is your chance if you want to take it. I can offer you a job as town marshal. D'you fancy that?'

Town marshal? Baxter was stunned, remembering Hank Judson as marshal of Lodge City, striding along Main to break up a fight, fearless with his long-barrelled Colt.

He gulped. 'You're joking?'

'No joke, Billy. I've had two offers, and I can't accept both. Two towns, Prospect and Oxbow, have each offered me the post of town marshal.'

'But you're an outlaw!'

'Sometimes. In some places.' The Cisco Kid shrugged. 'It's rarely so clear cut if you're known as a gunfighter. One lot reckon you're a badman; someone else wants you with them, as a law and order man to help keep the peace.

'These two towns are promoting themselves for state capital — and a lot of money will flow into whichever town is so named. Both want to get their seamy side cleaned up.'

'Marshal . . . ?' Baxter hesitated, wistful. 'I don't think I could.'

'Of course you can! It'll be easier than you think — my reputation guarantees very few will challenge you! They'll be expecting me, so why should they suspect a ringer? All you need to do is bluff. Bluff, Billy! Stare them down. Don't run off at the mouth — and collect the salary. That we split; a third to me and you keep the rest.'

Baxter felt a thrill along his nerves. To be the Cisco Kid, marshal of —

'Which town?' he asked, his breath coming faster.

The Kid smiled and tossed a coin. 'You call — heads you get Prospect, tails Oxbow.'

It came down heads and colour flushed Baxter's face: marshal of Prospect. 'I'll do it!'

The Kid nodded. 'Of course you will. Now, I'd better give you some training with that gun, in case you have to use it.'

He stood up and walked to a tree-trunk, took an ace of hearts from his shirt pocket and pinned it up. As he walked back, he whirled about and fired a snapshot from the hip.

Baxter stared. The heart in the centre of the card had a hole in it.

'Now you try, Billy.'

He tried. He fumbled his draw, jerked the trigger and missed the tree.

'Try again, slowly this time. Relax and put accuracy before speed. You can always hit your target if you don't hurry, and take deliberate aim. More would-be gunfighters die young through trying to be fast than from any other cause. In a shoot-out, the fast man will risk missing you. Then you hit him, and he doesn't get a second chance.'

Baxter drew a breath and calmed himself.

'Take all the time you need. Aim and fire . . . that's better.'

The Cisco Kid kept him at it and, as they travelled towards Prospect and Oxbow, Baxter continued target practice.

'You'll do — providing you remember not to rush things, and stay away from whiskey. A drunk gunfighter is a dead one.'

They came to a fork in the trail, and the Kid reined back. 'Good luck, partner.' He pointed. 'You take that way.' He nodded, smiling, and rode on alone. Billy Baxter watched till he became a dot on the horizon, then turned his horse and headed for Prospect.

2

Trouble in Prospect

The prairie extended to the horizon under a deep-blue sky. The air was still and hot. Baxter pulled the brim of his hat low to shade his eyes, and his horse plodded without enthusiasm; perhaps it missed the wagon, or its companions in harness. The faint track he was following suggested few travellers.

Alone, on his way to the town of Prospect, Baxter wondered what sort of reception he could expect, and how to handle it. It seemed hours and miles since breakfast and his stomach growled a reminder; it had gotten used to regular meals.

He looked up again after a weary way and realized something had changed. A dark smudge in the distance could only be a group of buildings, and he flicked the reins to encourage his mount.

Closer to town he recognized he was passing the local Boot Hill. He saw a row of wooden crosses and a burial party grouped around an open grave. A couple of men wore dark suits and serious expressions, the few others were in working clothes and bare-headed.

A grave-digger leaned on his spade and watched men lower a coffin into the hole as someone scattered earth over it.

A gaunt man spoke low words and a slight breeze carried them to Baxter.

'Born from the womb of woman and returned to the womb of the earth, a man can only expect trouble in this life, and this one sure found it. The moral of my sermon is simple: if you ain't quick on the draw, leave your gun at home. Amen.'

Chilled, Baxter shuddered and rode on, wondering who the dead man had been. What was he getting into? His horse was moving along briskly, faster than he wanted now, as his worry swelled out of all proportion. He felt tempted to turn back, to forget the marshal's job. Then he remembered the Cisco Kid had called him 'partner'. Shamed, he sat straighter in the saddle and went on.

He relived a memory: Hank Judson riding into a cowtown with the notion of taming it. Hank's mouth made a grim slit as his gaze searched for troublemakers; they'd learn soon enough not to fool with the fighting marshal . . .

Billy Baxter felt hollow inside and, despite the sun, his spine was an icicle. He reached a straggle of sod huts, wooden shacks and empty lots and, finally, a signboard that read:

Welcome to Prospect.
This is First Street.

It was wide and dust-filled with false-fronted saloons and stores lining each side. There were a few small houses with picket fences.

16

Further along, an office proudly claimed that *The Sentinel* Lives Here.

Till he reached the central crossroads there had been few people about and no one had taken more than a brief glance his way.

Now, on one corner outside an elegant saloon, a row of drinkers on a bench regarded him with interest. A hotel squatted opposite; on the third and fourth corners were the Emporium and a bank built of mud bricks. Beyond the crossroads the town died away quickly into shacks and log cabins on Second Street.

Baxter paused outside the saloon and called, 'Where's the livery?'

A thumb jerked. 'Behind the hotel, stranger.'

'Thanks.'

Before he could move off, another voice slurred, 'Bet you're the famous Cisco Kid. Bet you can't hit the silver dollar from where you're sitting. Bet you're not a betting man. Bet I can out-shoot yuh any time. Bet — '

The speaker lurched to his feet, coming down from the plankwalk to inch-thick dust.

Someone said, 'Take it easy, you fool. Somebody get the mayor.'

Baxter's pulse raced and he moistened his lips. He looked at the sign above the saloon; it probably was a silver dollar, he thought, and a damned small target at that distance.

Obviously the Cisco Kid would hit the mark easily — he remembered in time that he was the Kid and drew his revolver. It was a pity he was still in the saddle; shooting from horseback was something he hadn't practised.

He recalled the Kid's words, 'All you need to do is bluff' and lifted his revolver. He took his time, sighted carefully and squeezed the trigger.

Did his horse move a fraction? After he'd fired, he realized there had been three crows perched just above the dollar sign. Two flew away and the third dropped in the dust.

The drunk reeled back, his face a

pale shade of grey. 'Didn't mean nothing, stranger,' he muttered, and stumbled off.

The watchers appeared impressed so Baxter slid his gun into its holster.

A portly figure came rolling along First, puffing a little, white moustache reminding Baxter of a picture he'd seen of a walrus.

'Colonel Gus Whitney, mayor of Prospect — call me Gus, my boy. As fine a piece of shooting as I've seen — I doubt anyone's going to argue with the Cisco Kid.'

Baxter dismounted and Whitney pumped his hand. 'So glad you've accepted our offer.' Up close, Baxter could smell whiskey on the mayor's breath.

Another man came stalking towards them, gaunt of face and wearing a patched suit.

Whitney said, 'Jerry, meet our new marshal. Jerry Trumbo owns the *Sentinel* — give him a big write-up, Jerry.'

The newspaper editor nodded

brusquely. 'Naturally, Gus. You'll give me an interview, Kid?'

'Later. Right now I'd rather get my horse to a stable, wash up and eat.'

Mayor Whitney's voice boomed jovially. 'Of course, of course. Jerry, see to his horse, will you? This way, Kid.'

Baxter removed his saddle and pack and carried these as Whitney laid a plump white hand on his arm and directed him away from the crossroads and along Second Street.

'Here's the jail-house, with your office. There's a bunk you can use, and meals are provided by Stan's café.'

Whitney strode in and jerked open a desk drawer, brought out a metal badge and rubbed it on his cuff.

'Let me pin this on so folk know we have a peace officer at last. Er, fancy a drink? I usually have one about this time.'

Baxter shook his head. 'Thanks, but I don't indulge. I prefer to keep a clear head and a steady hand.'

The colonel sighed.

'I know what you mean. As an ex-army man myself, I know the temptation — you're absolutely right, sir, whiskey and straight shooting don't go together.'

A thought appeared to brighten his face.

'But when we're named state capital, things will be different. And yes, myself named state governor, cause for celebration then. Right now, your job is to keep the peace. More families are arriving all the time, women with kids making a home. The frontier's changing, and we need to change with it.

'We must prove we've put our gun-toting days behind us and are a law-abiding community. Know what I mean? Lay a revolver barrel alongside a troublemaker's skull and throw him in jail. In the morning, I'll fine him and that helps the town's coffers.' The mayor winked. 'If only I were younger . . .'

Baxter looked at the steel cage

behind the desk, with his bunk close by and wondered how much sleep he'd be getting.

'On the way in,' he said, 'I passed a funeral party and — '

Whitney said hastily, 'A shooting — our last, I hope. Just the sort of thing we're paying you to stop.'

'Who did the shooting?'

'Mueller, Roach's foreman. He'll need tactful handling.'

'Why's that?'

Whitney fluffed out his moustache. 'Mr Roach is the big rancher around here, and busy building himself an empire. He uses our largest store and his cowhands the Silver Dollar. If we upset Roach he could take his trade to Oxbow' — the mayor scowled — 'our rival in the race for state capital. But you'll read all about that in the *Sentinel*.'

Baxter nodded. 'So where's this café? My stomach says it's past time to eat.'

'Follow me.' Whitney led him outside and further along Second Street to a small shop with a hand-lettered sign: *Stan's Eats*.

Baxter stepped inside and Whitney, behind him, called, 'The new marshal, Stan,' and turned away. Baxter glimpsed his back as he hurried off.

Stan glared at him and snorted. 'The Cisco Kid, is it? Trust our mayor to hire a killer, then expect me to feed him on the cheap. You'll get the same as the prisoners and if you don't like that, go someplace else!'

Stan faced him, a small man with wispy grey hair; his arms were folded across a none-too-clean apron in a belligerent attitude.

The diner had five small tables, all empty. Baxter sat down at the nearest to the stove.

'I've been riding all day, Stan, and I'm starving. I'll eat whatever you put in front of me and be grateful. If you've a grudge going with the mayor, I don't have one with you.'

The cook relaxed slightly, still grumbling. 'I oughtn't to take it out on you, but that damned Gus annoys me. You'd think he was doing me a favour the way he insists I feed the prisoners, and then demands a cut price! And he's a relative.' He turned his head to spit through the doorway.

'A relative?'

'I'm ashamed to admit it, young fellar, but our Gus is like the rotten apple in a barrel — there's always one in every family, right? You read the print off'n this while I cook up something.'

Baxter took the copy of the *Sentinel* Stan handed him and glanced at the headline and opening paragraphs:

CATS' MEAT FOR WASHINGTON

The inhabitants of that hell-hole known as Oxbow are at it again! Regular readers know that our not-so-friendly rival is aiming to be state capital, despite being totally unsuited for this honour. Now we hear that their mayor, a store-keeper by the name of Neilson, is proposing to stand for state governor!

This is nothing less than criminal! We are informed on the best authority that this same Neilson sells cats' meat in his store and calls it prime steak! Without doubt, his supporters are beyond help from even the greatest brain doctor in the land!

SUPPORT MAYOR WHITNEY PROSPECT FOR STATE CAPITAL

For a moment, Baxter wondered how the Cisco Kid was getting on in Oxbow; then Stan put a large plate filled with meat and potatoes in front of him, and he stopped wondering and started eating.

Stan watched with growing satisfaction. 'That's what I like to see, a young 'un who knows how to put it away. I'll heat up some apple pudding.'

Baxter nodded, his mouth full.

The apple was dried and the pudding

25

crusty but still it went down. Stan brought a large tin cup and filled it with black coffee.

Baxter sat back and let out his belt a notch. 'Feels good.'

'Waal, maybe you won't be so bad as marshal . . . '

Baxter stared through the doorway where daylight was fading. 'Kind of quiet,' he said, his eyes beginning to close.

It had been a long day and he fancied a bed rather than the ground, and maybe a couple of blankets if the night turned chill.

Hoofbeats echoed, coming at a gallop. He heard excited yells and gunshots. Cowhands rode in from the range, milling in a mob outside the big saloon and calling loudly for whiskey.

'That'll be Roach's outfit,' Stan said. 'They figure to liven things up when they hit town.'

Baxter remembered the burial party. 'Will Mueller be with them?'

'Almost certain.'

Baxter felt a distinct chill, and sighed. It looked like being either a long night or a short life. Time to start earning his money. He stood up and adjusted the hang of his holster.

'Good luck,' Stan murmured.

Baxter moved outside. How did Hank Judson do it? He remembered a cover illustration ... with measured strides, calm and deliberate. Waal, he could try.

The Silver Dollar was a blaze of oil light. The shooting had stopped, but the roar of voices demanding whiskey grew louder and mingled with swearing and raucous singing. The volume of noise washed over a line of tethered cow ponies who'd heard it all before.

Baxter paused outside the batwings and drew air into his lungs. He loosened the revolver in its holster and wiped his hands down his pants. Then he pushed into the saloon.

Heads turned and the noise died away. Obviously the Cisco Kid was expected.

The crowd was composed mainly of

cowboys, with a few townsmen; a lone gambler turned cards over while waiting for customers. Wooden stairs led up to a balcony where a woman leaned on a railing, looking down.

Two men stood apart from those at the bar, one expensively dressed, the other wearing two revolvers low-slung. The cattleman and his foreman were talking with the saloon-keeper; he waited behind the bar wearing an embroidered vest and smoking a cheroot, his gaze on Baxter.

Mueller appeared tense, a killer on a leash waiting to be turned loose. He was broad across the chest and wore his dark hair long and loose about his shoulders.

Roach was short and bulky with the prominent hooked nose of a bird of prey; his hair was already thinning and he had the brooding air of a power-house. He looked the more dangerous of the two because he was obviously in command: Mueller was his chosen weapon.

Each held a glass of whiskey. Roach obviously enjoyed the taste; Mueller sipped cautiously.

Baxter began to feel an idiot just standing there. How would Hank Judson have acted? He forced his legs into motion, walking towards them. Mueller scowled.

Roach said quietly, 'Wait. The Cisco Kid isn't your usual drunk.' He made an easy smile. 'We're not looking for trouble if you're not, Marshal.'

Baxter forced a return smile. 'I'm intending to see trouble doesn't happen. The colonel wants a quiet town.'

'The colonel? You mean Gus . . . my crew get a little noisy at times, but there's no real harm in them.'

'I heard your foreman killed — '

'He was challenged,' Roach said quickly. 'He drew second. A case of self defence.'

'Naturally.'

It seemed a stand-off; then Mueller gestured with his glass. 'I guess we understand each other — name your poison.'

Baxter said, 'I don't drink,' and the foreman's scowl came back.

'Are you refusing to drink with me?'

Tension filled the air; then a stumpy man with bow legs tugged at Baxter's arm. 'If you're the marshal, I've got a complaint to make.'

Baxter transferred his attention. 'What kind of complaint? Who are you?'

'My name's Ferris, and I run a small ranch outside Prospect. My complaint's against Roach — he's been running off my cows.'

There was a shuffling of boots as men moved back from the small group at the bar. Mueller crouched, hands touching the butts of his guns.

Baxter warned, 'No gunplay in town,' and Roach laughed.

'Hold it, Carl. Time enough for that on the open range.'

Baxter glanced at Ferris; he was not a young man, his face as weathered as his hat. 'D'you have any proof of your statement?'

'Sure. Ride out with me, and I'll show yuh some brand-blotting.'

Roach swallowed his whiskey and pushed the glass at the saloon-keeper for a refill.

'Forget it, Ferris. This marshal's law ends at the town limits, and I figure he's smart enough to know he has no authority on my range.'

'It's not your range,' Ferris shouted.

Mueller regarded both Ferris and Baxter with cold fury. 'If I find either of yuh on Big R land I'll give you a bellyful of lead.'

Roach sipped his whiskey and smiled. 'No trouble, please, Marshal, or I'll have to take my business to Oxbow.'

Baxter felt certain Mayor Whitney wouldn't want that. 'Mr Roach, please make sure your men are under control while they're in town.'

He took a firm grasp of Ferris's arm. 'Outside,' he said.

He was aware it was only postponing

trouble, but he was still alive even if he'd never been so scared in his life. The bluff seemed to be working, but what if he were found out and challenged?

On First Street he told Ferris, 'Stay away from Roach's outfit,' and walked off. Sweat dried on him. The thought of how close he'd come to disaster made his knees tremble, and he wondered how the Kid was getting on.

3

The Viking

The Cisco Kid came into Oxbow just after dawn. He'd made a night camp and then followed the river, his mare fresh and frisky. From experience he'd learnt that late night hellions would be sleeping it off in the morning.

He rode quietly along Front Street, wondering where the river had gone. Obviously this stretch had once been a riverfront. Now the town buildings faced an expanse of dried mud where grass struggled to grow.

He paused at a horse trough and watched the shops opening; a man stood in the porch of a two-storey hotel, smoking a cheroot; one shop was labelled the Indepedent, a big sprawling saloon the Horseshoe; men in overalls with picks and shovels and mules were leaving town. Finally, his gaze settled on a double-fronted general merchandise store, Neilson's.

He urged the mare towards the store; it obviously catered for every need from a tin bath to shirts, from grocery provisions to guns and ammunition. He saw sacks and barrels and hams. And Erik Neilson was the one who'd signed the letter as mayor of Oxbow.

The Kid dismounted, hitched his mare and walked inside. Even this early there were a few customers being served, so he waited patiently.

Neilson was freshly shaved and eager for business; a big tough-looking Swede with short-cropped hair and massive hands.

'Help you?'

'Guess I'm here to help you,' the Kid drawled, and showed the letter offering him the job of town marshal. 'This finally caught up with me.'

Neilson looked him up and down, noting the revolver at his hip, the alert stance, the brown hands skilfully rolling a cigarette.

He nodded. 'You'll do. Don't think I can't handle troublemakers, but I've got a business to run, and — '

'Sure you can,' the Kid agreed, 'and so can I. But you can handle business and I can't.'

Neilson opened a cupboard behind the counter and rummaged till he found a badge; he tossed it to the Kid who caught it and pinned it to his shirt.

The new marshal lit his cigarette and blew out the match. 'Rowdy cowpunchers, is it?'

'Not usually. Roach's Big R outfit seldom visit us. It's miners. They make a strike and want to live it up. Good for business, but sometimes they get out of hand.

'This town's aiming to become the state capital — I'm hoping to be the first governor. You help keep a clean quiet place and there's a town lot for you.' Neilson hesitated briefly. 'That could be worth something in the future

— and, as governor, I could sign a pardon.'

The Kid stared hard at him. 'Meaning I wouldn't have to keep running?'

Neilson nodded brusquely. 'The jailhouse is just down the street. There's a bunk you can use, get your meals at — '

The Kid shook his head. 'That's not my style. I'll room at the hotel and eat there. Right now I've been riding too long and need to sit over a large meal. I could use an advance of salary.'

Neilson dipped his hand into the till and handed him a ten-dollar bill.

The Kid tucked it away in a shirt pocket, saluted casually and strolled outside. He finished his cigarette and ground the butt under his heel, walked his mare along to the high wooden building labelled HOTEL.

A lame boy on a stick waited outside the porch, looking hopefully at the marshal's badge. The Kid tossed him a coin and the mare's reins.

'See to my horse, son — tell the stableman to give her grain.'

He walked into the hotel, finding the dining-room by the smell of cooked food. Several men were at breakfast and eyed him warily. The Kid nodded casually to them and took a seat alone, with his back against a wall and a view of the door and window.

When a man in an apron bustled up, the Kid said, 'I'll be rooming and eating here. I'll take steak and I like a lot of it for each meal.'

'Sure thing, Marshal.' He laid a newspaper on the table. 'Our local.'

The Kid left it unopened; he'd look through it later, in the privacy of his room. He was more interested in the men of Oxbow who avoided his eye, hurried their meal and left.

A reputation, he mused, was a funny thing. Some ran from you; others hunted you; still others wanted to challenge you.

He sighed, remembering when he'd left home; sixteen, and it had been fun to hold up a stage. It had been an easy life until the day a passenger drew on him and he shot first and the man died. After that, life changed.

A life on the run was no longer carefree with money coming his way for a minimum of effort. Now he had a price on his head and bounty hunters on his trail. Wanted posters used the word 'outlaw'. Newspapers called him the Cisco Kid.

His steak came, rare and oozing blood, and he ate slowly. If he played his hand right, he might get a fresh start . . . an image of Billy Baxter suddenly popped into his head and his knife poised halfway to his mouth, a lump of steak speared to the end.

How good was the youngster at bluffing? Did he have the men of Prospect convinced he was the Cisco Kid? Would he withdraw from the marshal's job before he, too, killed somebody?

He slid the piece of steak into his mouth and chewed thoughtfully. Maybe the bounty hunters would mistake Billy for himself and take the pressure off? Suppose they killed Baxter and claimed he was the Kid? Then he could vanish . . . Billy, as a sacrifice.

He finished his meal and used a pick between his teeth; the Kid's smile had a touch of the wolf about it.

After two cups of coffee he asked about a room and followed the hotelman upstairs to a back room. He dumped his kit on the bed, opened the window and looked out.

The street behind the hotel was rapidly developing into a main thoroughfare, with a wide road and plankwalks. Shops were springing up: he saw a baker's shop, a small general store and a milliner's. He glimpsed hills beyond.

He stretched out on the bed and unfolded the *Oxbow Independent*.

MURDER IN PROSPECT!

Once again the rowdy element has taken over the town — yet another citizen has been shot dead! And this trouble hotspot intends to stand for state capital? Ridiculous!

Our would-be rival is no more than an outlying district of Hell, and its mayor a cross between a hyena and a donkey — as well as being a compulsive liar!

By contrast, we here in Oxbow will shortly have as town marshal, a famous gunfighter, to ensure our town remains a hive of peaceful activity.

SUPPORT MAYOR NEILSON!
OXBOW FOR STATE CAPITAL

The Kid smiled: Billy could be having an interesting time. He lay back on the bed and smoked a cigarette; he ought to show himself around town, let people see he was on the job.

Downstairs, he ambled along the boardwalk, first stop the jail; it was small but solid, with an iron cage at the back, empty at the moment. He looked through the desk and found a sheaf of Wanted notices — and carefully destroyed one that had his picture on it.

He strolled out, noting saloons and private houses and shops.

Past the *Independent* office, he saw a young woman riding a chestnut stallion. They made a striking combination. He admired first the horse, and then its rider: she was tall and strong and held herself proudly, fair hair flowing like a banner, a Viking of a woman.

She saw him at the same time and swung easily from the saddle to hitch her mount to the nearest post.

'You must be the Cisco Kid — welcome to Oxbow!' She gave him a dazzling smile. 'I'm Val Neilson — obviously you've met my father. Waal' — she ran an eye over him; a calculating eye when it came to sizing up men — 'you look like you can handle the marshal's job.' Her tone was admiring.

'I think so,' the Kid drawled.

'We'll meet again,' she said, turning away. 'I'll make sure of it. Right now

41

I've got an errand.'

She moved off with long strides and the Kid watched till she disappeared through a doorway. He squared his shoulders: some woman! Time to smarten up he thought, rubbing a hand over a bristly chin. He was whistling as he headed for the barber's shop for a hair cut, bath and shave.

But he reminded himself, a bit of sparking only, strictly no strings attached . . .

It was a spruced-up Cisco Kid, smelling faintly of bay rum, who patrolled the streets as evening closed in. He was left in no doubt that Oxbow was a mining town; miners, dirt-covered and carrying their tools, swarmed in for food and entertainment; some with nuggets and others with small leather bags.

The townsfolk closed their doors and drew heavy curtains across windows. Oil lamps blazed from saloons; fiddles played and whiskey flowed after the dining-rooms shut.

The Horseshoe was a riot of noise as he patrolled the town and he quickly realized he wouldn't be popular if he tried to stop the fun. There was a fine line between lifting the miners' money and shops getting wrecked and citizens hurt.

He figured it would be enough to show his face in the rowdiest saloons; a hint to keep trouble non-lethal. One of the women winked at him, but he ignored her.

Then, as he was coming back from the far end of town, two figures reeled out of the Horseshoe. It looked as if they had been pushed outside. They were both miners, swearing and bawling threats; each carried a long-handled shovel and lunged at the other with violence in mind.

The Kid started towards them.

* * *

Val Neilson sat close to the open window of her room above the store,

43

looking down on Front Street and listening to the sounds of evening. She was young enough to want to join in; old enough to know these roughnecks were not the kind to interest her. They thought first of gold, then whiskey and, when drunk, a woman. There were times when she found it difficult to put up with their attempts to court her.

Oil lamps made flickering shadows, and she could hear singing and laughter; soon there would be a brawl; it was all so predictable.

As she watched, two men stumbled through the batwings of the Horseshoe, by their dress, obviously miners. They cursed and threatened each other. What was different from previous fights she'd seen was that each carried a long-handled spade which they swung with murderous intent.

As the first lunged and missed, glass tinkled as it struck a window. The other bawled, 'Steal my claim, will yuh? I'll show you what — '

'Your claim! You lying bastard; for

that I'm going to separate your head from your shoulders!'

Val realized both were whiskey-serious and swinging their long blades with a force that could maim or kill. The first man struck home, cleaving flesh to the bone; a gaping wound sprayed blood.

The injured man staggered, howling like a stuck pig. The victor rushed in for the kill, but missed, and the pair waltzed around like punch-drunk boxers.

Val frowned. Unless someone stopped them this fight could end in murder.

A shovel flailed again and —

She saw the Kid coming with quickened strides, drawing his revolver. He moved in close to the victorious miner and laid the barrel of his gun alongside his skull. He dropped, and the injured miner tried to hit him while he was down.

The new marshal jabbed a revolver into his back.

'Quieten down and start walking. You can bed down in the jail and sleep it off. You'll feel differently in the morning.'

He returned minutes later, picked up the fallen miner by his ankles and dragged him through the dust to the jailhouse.

Oxbow suddenly went quiet; then Val saw Dr Paul carry his black bag to the jail.

Her blood pulsed as she flushed hot and a thrill coursed through her. She'd felt attracted to the Kid when she first saw him; now he'd proved himself.

At last, she thought, a man she could get seriously interested in. Tomorrow she'd ride to Prospect to confide in her friend Dot.

* * *

The two men riding the faint track that led to Prospect were dressed in clothes the worse for long wearing. Their faces, beneath unshaven whiskers, held the common stamp of brutality. Both were heavily armed and experienced in the use of their weapons; a townsman would have turned up his nose at their smell.

Their mounts had been ridden almost to exhaustion because they were not the kind to spare horse-flesh with the end of the chase in sight. Neither liked the other, but they'd made a truce for however long it took to nail the Cisco Kid; each considered him too dangerous to tackle alone. That didn't mean they trusted each other.

'Bracket him,' grunted Bony, the stringy one. 'Get him between us so he can't cover both of us at the same time. That way one of us will get him for sure.'

The heavyweight, Joe, brooded for a moment, using his greasy hat to whisk away horse-flies.

'You wouldn't be figuring to hide behind me? I want you out in front where I can see yuh.'

Bony scowled. 'We'll each take our

chances when the time comes. One of us will be sure to collect.'

'Yeah,' Big Joe muttered under his breath. 'And I'll make sure that one is me.'

'It's a fifty-fifty split,' Bony reminded his reluctant partner.

The two bounty hunters rode a while in silence, each planning to collect the blood money on the Kid's head for himself.

4

Which Kid?

Billy Baxter tried not to show how nervous he was at being interviewed by Jerry Trumbo, owner-editor of Prospect's *Sentinel*. He had to be careful how he answered questions so as not to give the deception away. All he knew about the Cisco Kid's life was what he'd read in a newspaper back in San Francisco.

The editor didn't seem so formidable with his coat and tie off and his shirt sleeves rolled up. He adjusted a pair of spectacles on his nose as he sat at a desk with a pad of paper and pen and ink.

The office was small, stacked with sheets of blank paper and smelt of printing ink. Trumbo's hands showed he'd been wrestling with an oil-can on

49

the hand press he used to print the news.

'Now, Marshal, people are interested in your family, home life and how you got started as a gunfighter. So just a few questions to give you the idea. Let's see . . . you came from a well-to-do family — that always goes down well — the handsome daredevil black sheep . . . right?'

'I suppose so,' Baxter said slowly. The Kid hadn't struck him quite that way.

'And, of course, you started college, but quit to look for adventure?'

Baxter nodded.

'And you practised with a revolver till you were a dead shot and quick on the draw? And when you held up your first stagecoach it was for pure devilment . . . ' Trumbo kept jotting down notes as if Baxter had given these answers, his expression perfectly serious. Suddenly he paused to stare at Baxter's gunbelt. 'Only one revolver?'

Baxter said drily, 'One is usually enough.'

'Of course,' Trumbo said hastily. 'I didn't mean ... How many, er — notches! Ah, now I see it's a new Colt. How many in your old gun? That's the sort of thing people like to know. Five? Six? More?'

'I don't exactly recollect.'

'Modest, too,' Trumbo murmured. 'Ten is a nice round number,' the editor decided, scribbling away. 'Our readers expect certain conventions — just leave it to me. I know what they like!'

He was still devising the Kid's life when Baxter got up quietly and left, appreciating that the editor would do better without him.

Outside the *Sentinel* office he paused a moment to get his breath back. Jerry Trumbo had put him in a bit of a daze. He remembered the Kid's advice, 'Don't run off at the mouth', and laughed.

He saw two women walking towards him. One carried a basket and he vaguely recognized her as a shopper he'd seen around town.

The other was tall and statuesque and strode along the boardwalk as he imagined a conquering Viking might, fair hair streaming out behind her. Magnificent, he thought, stunned. And young, about his own age.

Billy Baxter's mouth opened but no sound came out. He stood riveted, like a victim waiting to be sacrificed.

★　★　★

Val Neilson rode towards Prospect in a state of great excitement. At night, she'd been restless, thinking of the Cisco Kid; and when, finally, she slept, she dreamed about him.

That morning over breakfast, her father had asked if anything was wrong. She'd made the excuse of wanting to talk to Dot — her only woman friend since her mother died — and he'd stopped asking questions.

She saddled Rusty and let him gallop. As the miles fled beneath the chestnut's hoofs she felt like singing. Life was good.

The blacksmith's shop in Prospect was on Second Street, not far from the crossroads, and Val dismounted and removed the saddle. She carried it inside.

'Hi, Dan. Is Dot about?'

The smith finished hammering a shoe into shape before answering. 'Hello, Val. You'd best hurry — she's going shopping.'

Val went to the back of the smithy and through a doorway that led into a small house. She'd always felt comfortable with Dot, a friend of her mother's; although older and married, she treated Val as an adult and they talked woman to woman.

The smith's buxom wife was removing her apron as she arrived. 'Val, I wasn't expecting you today. Is anything wrong?'

'No, something's right — I've met a real man, at last.'

Dot smiled. 'It had to happen

sometime. I'm glad for you.'

'He's our new marshal, and he's called the Cisco Kid.'

Dot picked up her shopping basket, paused, and stared at her. '*Your* marshal?'

'Yes, in Oxbow. What's wrong?'

'We've got a new marshal here, and he calls himself the Cisco Kid.'

'No, Dot, you must have misheard. There can't be two of them, and mine makes my heart beat faster whenever I see him.'

'It's odd, but ours is usually about town, so we can ask him what's going on.'

They left the house and, as they reached the crossroads, Roach was hitching a horse outside the bank. The rancher stepped directly in their path and raised his hat.

'Miss Neilson, Val, it's good to see you again. I hope you'll take up my offer soon to visit the Big R. There's plenty to see, and the house really does need a woman's touch.'

Val remained cool. Roach was an important man, and had shown an interest in her before. She didn't much like him; and, contrasting his hooked nose and thinning hair with the Kid's physique, she positively disliked him.

'Thanks for the offer,' she said stiffly. 'Right now I want words with your marshal.'

'Not my marshal. Another time then. I, too, have business to transact.' He nodded to Dot and stepped inside the bank.

He must be one of the few who need a bank, Val thought as they walked on.

Dot said, 'There he is now — coming out of the newspaper office.'

Val stared critically. 'The one with his mouth open? *That* calls itself the Cisco Kid? Looks more like a boy playing hookey from school — the real Cisco Kid is a *man*!'

Prospect's lawman closed his mouth as they reached him. He smiled and lifted his Stetson. 'Good-day, ladies.'

Val said, 'I hear you're calling

yourself the Cisco Kid. Is that true?'

For a moment, he appeared startled. 'That's right, ma'am, that's how I'm generally known.'

Val gave a snort of disgust. 'You're a liar! I'm from Oxbow so I've met the real Kid. You're not even a pale imitation — just some kind of cheap crook using his name. You should be ashamed to pretend you're someone you're not!'

He seemed taken aback by her attack, but recovered. 'I assure you, ma'am, that I'm the Cisco Kid. You can ask Colonel Whitney — '

Val barked a laugh. 'Colonel? I don't think so . . . more likely sergeant, if that.'

'Waal, I don't really know much about his army career, but I'm called the Cisco Kid. Sounds to me like your man in Oxbow may be an imposter.'

Sparks flashed from Val's eyes; her hands knotted into fists.

'Imposter! I shall repeat your accusation when I get back — then we'll see

56

who's the fake. My advice to you is to get on your horse and get out of town.' Her voice held a sneer. 'I hope you're as good at running as you are at lying.'

He touched his hat as she turned away. 'Sure sorry to hear you say that, ma'am.'

Val stalked off along the boardwalk, her face flushed.

Dot smiled and said, 'I do believe you've made another conquest!'

* * *

They sat in a small saloon in Prospect, close by the door and looking out on First Street. It was a shadowy saloon and they were just two riders taking it easy. They had the place to themselves almost, sitting quietly with a bottle and two glasses and washing the dust from their throats. They were content to stay out of the sunlight.

Big Joe wore a worried frown. 'D'yuh reckon she's right, Bony?'

The stringy one studied Prospect's

marshal with some care. 'He does look kind of young,' he admitted.

The blonde woman's tirade had disturbed both men and Bony brought a Wanted notice from a pocket and unfolded it. He compared the picture, feature by feature, with the young man who called himself the Cisco Kid.

'There's no point in killing the wrong man,' Joe said. 'Nobody's going to pay us for that — apart from folk not taking kindly to us for shooting their lawman.'

The two women turned away and still the marshal stood there, staring after them.

'I guess she's right,' Bony said. 'This one is too young to be the real thing. The Kid looks years older in this picture. 'Oxbow', she said. Reckon we'll ride that way since she seemed sure the Oxbow Kid is the one we're hunting.'

Joe grunted. 'Let's finish this bottle first.'

5

Lone Raider

'Another conquest!'

All the way back to Oxbow, Dot's words rang in her ears. Val was so furious her face was red and she quirted Rusty, something she rarely did. The stallion responded with another burst of speed.

All her young life she'd had men falling for her; it was something she took for granted. But that weak-kneed apology for a man? There was something about the fake Cisco Kid that got under her skin. She despised him . . . some conquest!

When she arrived on Front Street, she halted with a flourish at the jailhouse, dropped the reins and stormed inside. The Cisco Kid had his boots on the desk and his Stetson tipped to the back of his head; he was rolling cigarettes and lining them up like soldiers on parade.

Val snapped, 'I've just been visiting in Prospect — and the marshal there claims he's the Cisco Kid.'

'That so?' The Kid looked interested. 'How's he doing?'

Val might have been a volcano about to explode. 'Obviously he's an imposter! You must do something about him.'

'Like what?'

'Call him out!'

The Kid finished making a cigarette and stuck it behind his ear. He seemed amused.

'No need to get excited, ma'am. Since I got this reputation, any number of would-be badmen have held up a stage or robbed a bank — and used my name so I get the blame.'

'That's terrible! All the more reason to stamp on this fraud.'

'This one's a marshal, you say? So he's not doing me any harm. Forget it.' The Kid glanced through the open

60

doorway. 'Best see to your horse.'

Val glared at him in frustration. Men! Sometimes she didn't understand how their minds worked . . . if they had minds. She turned on a heel and stalked out. Feeling guilty, she walked Rusty to the stable, rubbed him down and gave him a feed.

It was not far to the office of the *Independent*, and she strode in, banging the doors.

The editor — named Holland, so everyone called him Dutch — was setting type on his printing machine. He had a roly-poly figure and an air of not quite belonging to this world.

'Don't bother banging the door on the way out — just go away, whoever you are.' He spoke without looking up.

'Do you want me to tell Dad that?'

Dutch paused to glance around. 'Oh, it's you, Val.'

They both knew her father put money into the *Independent* to keep it going, to boost Neilson and Oxbow's chance at state capital.

'What is it?'

'There's a new marshal in Prospect, and he claims to be the Cisco Kid.'

Dutch's fingers ripped out type and began to reset, composing as he went along. 'Keep talking.'

'He further claims that our marshal, here in Oxbow, is an imposter!'

'Huh,' grunted Dutch, 'I'll soon fix him!'

When Val finished, though she felt better, she was still restless; there must be more she could do to demolish the idiot who pretended to be the man she intended to marry.

★　★　★

Carl Mueller walked into Roach's office at the Big R ranch-house and found his boss staring at a pile of paperwork. Bills, he supposed from the expression on his face. He waited, standing, hat in hand. Roach liked that.

The rancher finally looked up. 'Yes? What is it?' He sounded testy.

'The cattle are coming along fine, but water's going to be a problem. Unless we get rain soon, we're going to lose some — the river level's lower every day.'

Roach's face began to resemble a thundercloud. He was never happy with the idea of losing anything. He was one of the world's grabbers.

'I have noticed, Carl, and plan to do something about it.'

Like what? the foreman thought. Bribe an Indian medicine man to perform a rain dance?

The boss seemed broody these days — too intent on having the Neilson bitch here. The ranch house was big and bare.

Mueller's smile was edged with frost. He, too, had plans for her but there was no hurry. Anticipation, he'd learnt, was a major factor in satisfaction.

'Another thing,' he said. 'That piebald's gone missing again. A wandering horse ain't worth anything. Never there when needed, just a nuisance. Maybe we should get rid of it.'

Roach stared at him as if he'd gone mad. 'Get rid of a horse I paid money for?'

Mueller suppressed his amusement. 'We could plant it on Ferris,' he suggested.

'That's different . . . ' Roach considered hanging the other rancher as a horse-thief and taking his cattle. 'Not yet,' he decided reluctantly.

'You afraid of a two-bit marshal?'

'No. The sheriff will be riding this way — it's getting towards election time again. But I like the idea; let it simmer for a while.'

★   ★   ★

Outside the bank the midday sun blazed and dogs slept in the shade. Most people were either eating or taking a siesta.

Arnold, Prospect's sole bank clerk, sat behind the counter, eating off a dish

64

supplied by Stan's café; his boss dined at the hotel. Through the wide open doors he had a partial view of the crossroads and an empty boardwalk.

Might just as well shut the doors, he thought, for all the business we're likely to do. Then he heard a single rider come down Second Street, slow and easy.

He felt a mild curiosity but it was too hot to move to satisfy it. He continued eating till the rider stopped to hitch his mount just out of view. It seemed whoever it was might have business with the bank. The visitor paused a moment in the doorway, a wide-brimmed hat shadowing the face, and brought up a neckerchief to act as a mask.

Arnold was still a young man even if he was starting a beer belly; but he froze when he looked into the muzzle of a revolver. The bore appeared frighteningly large.

The masked raider threw an empty sack at him. 'If you want to go on living, fill that with money; notes, coins, whatever you've got handy, and be quick about it.'

Arnold swallowed to clear his mouth. 'Are you trying to give me indigestion? Reckon you're a stranger, so I'll tell yuh — our town marshal is the Cisco Kid and you won't want him on your trail.'

The gun barrel jerked menacingly. 'Your marshal means nothing to me. Fill that sack before I fill you plumb full of lead!'

The voice was muffled, and Arnold started to obey. He worked slowly, picking out small denomination notes and small coins, and hoping someone would call at the bank.

'Faster. I'm losing patience!'

Arnold mumbled, 'I'm going as fast as I can.'

'Tie the neck of the sack.'

The raider grabbed the sack of money and backed towards the door, revolver still pointed at the clerk.

'Don't try to follow me and don't shout. I'm a dead shot.'

Arnold took another mouthful of food. He got up and moved towards the door and watched the raider tie the sack to the saddle-horn, swing aboard a piebald horse and use spurs.

Then he ran outside, shouting, 'Bank raid! Stop him! Robbery — get the marshal!'

A couple of sleepy idlers on the bench outside the Silver Dollar came to their feet, firing wildly after the lone raider, crouched low and galloping out of town.

By the time Billy Baxter arrived, the masked robber was a speck in a cloud of dust. Someone brought his horse from the stable and he climbed into the saddle. An argument started as to whether the horse was Roach's piebald.

The banker came from the hotel dining-room, wiping his mouth with a napkin. 'Go get my money back, Marshal!'

There was a shout of encouragement as Baxter set off after the robber. He half-expected a posse to join him but the crowd moved into the shade to discuss the robbery. After all, it wasn't their money and the marshal got paid to risk his neck.

Baxter settled to the chase, urging his horse after the distant quarry; the outlaw seemed to be heading for a range of hills. He pressed his horse for greater speed but the animal was reluctant. It was more used to hauling a wagon.

Of course, Hank Judson would never have this kind of problem. He'd have been on the spot with a couple of deputies and the hold-up man would be on the ground riddled with lead.

Real life, Baxter reflected, didn't measure up to the dime novels he'd read. Instead, he'd been about to start on Stan's steak-and-onion pie and, right now, his stomach felt twice as empty.

Gradually Baxter fell further behind and, by the time he reached the base of the foothills and looked up at a fringe of trees, he was alone.

He reined back, listening; somewhere hoofs echoed faintly and he headed in that direction. He saw no one and paused to listen again. He didn't even hear a hoofbeat this time.

Somewhere in these hills, he'd been told, miners from Oxbow were digging for gold, but he couldn't find one to ask about his quarry. He wondered if the raider could possibly be a miner.

He dismounted and searched for tracks but the few scuff marks he saw were meaningless; he'd no experience of tracking. Perhaps he was on part of Big R's range; could the robber be one of Roach's crew?

Finally he admitted he'd lost the masked raider, who obviously knew the lie of the land. He rode slowly back to Prospect.

A reception committee waited for him, with Colonel Gus Whitney prominent. The mayor demanded, 'Have you brought back the stolen money?'

Jerry Trumbo pushed to the front, his

expression eager. 'Did you kill the bank robber?'

Someone else asked, 'Who was it? Anybody we know?' Baxter dismounted wearily and surrendered the reins to a waiting stableboy.

'Whoever it was got away, with the money. I never saw his face but he sure knows the land around here better than I do. He had no difficulty losing me.'

Whitney's ruddy face turned a sickly white. 'That isn't good enough! This is your fault — this is just the sort of thing you were hired to prevent.'

He tweaked his moustache in his excitement.

'One of Roach's lot,' a voice at the back muttered. 'Reckon it was his piebald.'

The mayor ignored this comment. 'At least we can be certain who's behind it. The people of Oxbow! They'll be saying we can't protect investors' money — and inviting our investors to put their money in the bank at Oxbow! You've got to do something about this,

Marshal — it's a serious matter.'

'I'll do something,' Baxter promised.

'Can you say you've a lead to follow?' Trumbo asked, opening his notebook. 'Give me a quote I can print.'

Someone laughed. 'I'll give you a quote, Jerry. If Roach's money ain't in the bank when he wants it, there'll be hell to pay!'

Whitney looked longingly in the direction of the Silver Dollar. 'I feel the need for a drink coming on . . . what will you do now, Marshal?'

Baxter began to walk towards Stan's café. 'Get outside some steak-and-onion pie!'

6

'No Lynching in Oxbow!'

Earl was eating a stale pie he'd got for half-price from the baker's shop on Back Street. His leg hurt more than usual today, so he sat on a wooden step to rest; usually he hobbled around to earn his keep, a nickel here, two bits there.

He sat in the shade, alone except for a dog as thin as he was. Most people avoided looking directly at a cripple, but not the dog; it waited patiently for a few crumbs with its tongue hanging out.

It was a quiet time, the shops almost empty. When he heard the slow walk of hard-ridden horses stirring the dust, he used his stick to struggle upright. Two riders came quietly into Oxbow.

He rarely missed a chance to earn a

few coins and, as they drew level, called, 'Stable your horses?'

The heavyweight only scowled as they passed by. The stringy one snapped, 'Clear off, boy, before yuh get hurt.'

He watched them to the corner of the street, then hobbled after them. They stopped outside a small saloon that only a few out-of-luck miners used. They hitched their weary mounts and went inside. At the bar they got a bottle of whiskey and two glasses.

They chose a table near the window, where they could see who was passing on the plankwalk, yet hardly be noticed. Suspicious, Earl settled again to keep watch on the newcomers, the dog beside him. Maybe the marshal would want to know about them.

★ ★ ★

The Cisco Kid was feeling pleasantly relaxed and at peace with the world. Val obviously had no idea he was responsible for Billy Baxter's presence in

73

Prospect; and the marshal's job in Oxbow was a cinch. A few drunken miners were no problem.

But it paid to show himself around town as darkness came, to let the mayor and council see he was taking the job seriously. For the time being, he was content to wear a badge and draw a regular income.

The evening was warm and dry as he patrolled Back Street, keeping to the shadows and pausing before crossing lighted areas. He wasn't expecting trouble, but neither was he careless; a careless gunfighter had a short life-span.

The baker's shop and the milliner's were in darkness; light shone from saloons, just starting to warm up as miners got back from their diggings.

He was not sure what alerted him. He was about to pass a side alley next to the hardware store when his ears tingled.

He checked his forward motion and, without conscious thought, hunched over to make himself a smaller target. A gunshot echoed and a bullet whip-cracked close enough for him to feel it cut the air. He glimpsed a vague figure in the alleyway and winged a shot that way.

He heard a startled cry behind him. 'Look out, Marshal — there's another one!'

The Kid whirled about, thinking, two men bracketing him. He crouched in shadow, cold-eyed. The second man was a heavyweight and, cursing, grabbed a boy — the lame one, he realized as a stick clattered to the wooden boards — to use as a shield.

The Kid's lip curled. He watched a gunhand appear from behind the boy and laughed as he fired a snapshot. His slug struck the gunman's hand and shattered the bones.

The would-be killer screamed his agony and hurled the boy violently to the ground. Behind him, the Kid heard urgent hoofbeats; the first gunman was riding for his life.

The Kid let him go and walked to where the lame boy lay in the dust with the gunman kicking him. He pushed the man back and sneered, 'Some hero, you are!'

He picked up the boy's stick and helped him up. 'Are you hurt bad, son?'

'Not me, Marshal. I'm used to kicks and curses.'

'What do they call yuh?'

'Earl.'

'Waal, Earl, you've done me a favour. If anyone picks on you in future, you tell them you're a friend of the Cisco Kid.'

'I'll surely do that, Marshal!'

The Kid turned his attention to the wounded gunman. 'Start walking — I'm locking you in our jail overnight.'

'What about my hand?'

'Reckon you won't be pulling a gun with that one.' The Kid prodded him with his revolver. 'Step along smartly.'

A few men appeared from the

saloons, including Dutch Holland with his notebook. 'What's happening? We heard shots.'

The Kid pushed his prisoner to keep him moving. 'Nothing much — ask Earl.'

The boy was enthusiastic and Dutch got a front page story for the *Independent*.

In the jailhouse, the Kid opened the iron cage at the rear and pushed his prisoner inside. He went through the gunman's pockets and took what money he had and transferred it to his own pocket.

'That's stealing.'

'That's what the Cisco Kid is good at.'

'I want a doctor — '

The Kid shook his head sadly. 'Can't advise that.'

'Why not? It hurts.'

'Our Dr Paul is an ex-army surgeon — a sawbones — and he likes to amputate.'

'Jeez, no thanks!'

The Kid locked the cell door, lit an oil lamp and sat at his desk ignoring the moans of the injured man. He rolled and lit a cigarette as he brought a bunch of Wanted notices from a drawer. He held each one up in turn, comparing the pictures with his prisoner.

'What yuh doing?'

'Looking for your picture.'

'You won't find me there — you know damn well I'm a bounty man!'

'Do I?'

The Kid picked out one notice and studied it carefully. 'This ain't a bad match. Says here you're Louis Irvine and wanted for cattle rustling.'

'You can't frame me like that — you're the one who's wanted!'

'Can't I? I'm the one wearing a lawman's badge . . . '

★ ★ ★

After a generous helping of beef-and-onion pie — reheated for him personally

— Billy Baxter began to feel better. It helped that Stan seemed to admire him.

'Never thought I'd see an officer of the law put away grub the way you do. Thought they was all highly strung folk with stomach trouble. Try this special, will yuh?'

Stan placed another pie in front of Baxter, who loosened his belt and used a knife to cut the crust.

'Peach!' he exclaimed in delight.

'Dried, of course, but it makes a change from the usual.'

Baxter attacked the fruit and a pint of coffee and sat back. His fear of being found out and challenged shrivelled and hid in a corner of his brain; he felt expansive.

'What happened?' Stan asked, taking off his apron. He sat in a chair opposite and filled his pipe. 'Who was it robbed the bank?'

'At the moment I've no idea. A local man, obviously, because he lost me easily among the hills.'

'You'll nail him, Kid,' the cook said

confidently. 'A lawman who eats like you can't fail!'

Baxter's confidence grew; someone had faith in him. He remembered a dime novel in which Hank Judson faced a similar situation. The fighting marshal always knew what to do — he'd gone straight to the guilty man and arrested him.

He sat over a refill of coffee while Stan smoked and watched the changing expressions on his face.

Baxter thought, the Cisco Kid would know what to do too, and his face cleared; he'd ride to Oxbow and consult him.

'You've got it!' Stan exclaimed when Baxter asked him how to get to Oxbow.

★ ★ ★

Yellow oil lamps threw shadows on Front Street and the sounds of saloons livening up reached the jail-house. The Cisco Kid strolled to the door and looked and listened. Behind him, in the cage, the wounded bounty hunter continued to curse his partner.

'Damn that yellow rat Bony for quitting on me . . . leaving me here to rot while he makes a getaway!'

The Kid ignored him. He supposed he ought to be out patrolling, but he'd had enough excitement for one night. The shadows were dark out there; and the rising noise signified that Earl's story was developing with each telling.

He considered possibilities and, on impulse, picked up the cell key and unlocked the door. 'Move out!'

The bounty man didn't jump at the offer; he appeared to be suspicious. 'Why? What are you up to?'

The Kid drew his revolver.

'Maybe I should just shoot yuh when you try to escape . . . I'm turning you loose because I don't like the way the town's getting excited. I figure a crowd of miners drinking whiskey will turn into a mob — a lynch mob — and the mayor won't like that. I can hear him

81

plain as your face: 'No lynching in Oxbow!'

'What he wants is a peaceful town, so keep quiet and walk in the shadows and use back-streets. I don't want anyone to see yuh.'

The Kid turned out the lamp and paused at the door, listening to the buzz of voices from the saloons. He pushed his prisoner outside.

'Keep moving. I figure the crowd's getting worked up over the way you treated that crippled boy, and I don't see how I can hold them off if they catch up. They'll surely stretch your neck.'

The big bounty man moved a bit faster, freezing when a board creaked, walking on tiptoe, sweating where a shadow moved.

When they reached the edge of the town, the Kid said, 'Just keep walking till you reach those hills.'

'But I ain't got a horse, a gun, nothing.'

'You've got a pair of legs . . . '

The bounty man, holding his crippled hand and swearing, walked into the darkness.

The Kid waited till he could no longer see or hear him, then holstered his gun and strolled back to Front Street. He was smiling, figuring that neither bounty hunter would bother him again.

7

Cattle Thieves

Billy Baxter's horse was moving along slowly as he approached Oxbow, as if protesting against being ridden twice in one day. He had no difficulty finding the town; he'd set off in daylight and Stan's directions were clear enough. After the sun went down he rested till moonrise and then set off again.

When he reached Front Street he stopped the first person he met to ask, 'Where can I find your marshal?'

A miner peered at him, saw his badge and burst out laughing.

'That Neilson gal purely stirs things up — have you come to challenge the Cisco Kid? I'd sure like to see that!'

He turned towards the lawman's office and saw it was in darkness. 'Try the hotel. If he isn't there, I guess he'll be patrolling. Here, you can have this — I've finished with it.'

The miner pressed a copy of the *Independent* into Baxter's hand and walked on, chuckling.

The saloons were doing a lively trade and Baxter dismounted and hitched outside the Horseshoe, near the hotel. Oil light blazed from a window and he stepped close to read:

We hear from an unusually reliable source that Prospect's marshal has the bare-faced gall to call himself after our own marshal. Further, this lying son-of-a-bitch claims that our very own Cisco Kid is an imposter. Garbage!

We say, crawl back under the stone you came from, cheat and swindler — or face the guns of the one and only Kid in a showdown!

Baxter supposed this was Val's work, but why she should use such language he didn't understand. He walked into

85

the hotel; the door of the dining-room was open and he saw the Cisco Kid relaxing with a cup of coffee.

'Billy! Come and join me.' The Kid saw the newspaper he was carrying, and laughed. 'That Val, she doesn't pull any punches — guess you must have made an impression on her.'

Baxter's face reddened.

'Get you going, did she, Billy? Waal, she's chasing me so you can forget her — maybe you'll come in handy later, when I duck out.'

Baxter sat down, reached for a cup and poured himself a coffee from a jug. He got his breath back and started to speak, but the Kid hushed him.

'Later, in my room.'

Upstairs, looking out on Back Street, Baxter heard saloons going full blast with laughter and fiddle music and dancing.

The Kid grinned. 'Rumour says you had a bit of excitement in Prospect.'

Baxter nodded. 'Somebody robbed

the bank and I lost him. I don't know what to do.'

'There's not much you can do without a good tracker. If it's a local man, wait till someone starts spending more than usual.'

'The mayor wants action.'

The Kid shrugged. 'So give him something else to worry about.'

'Such as?'

'Waal now . . .' The Kid's eyes lit up. 'I remember a name on a Wanted notice I happened to look at recently: Louis Irvine. He's wanted for rustling cattle — and someone like him just quit town. You'll have a notice back in Prospect.'

The Kid began to pace the room, excited. 'This is what we'll do . . . run off a bunch of steers and, when the complaint comes in, you mention this rustler so he gets the blame. That way, your mayor will have an angry rancher on his back to take his mind off the bank job.'

It was obvious he considered this a

joke, but Baxter wasn't so sure. 'Suppose something goes wrong?'

'Stop worrying, Billy — things go wrong all the time. You wanted adventure and here it is.' The Kid looked him over critically. 'Take that badge off and put it in your pocket. We don't want that coming loose and someone finding it on the range.'

When they went downstairs, he examined Baxter's horse. 'You need something with more go in it — and I happen to have acquired a spare. Hard-used, but rested and fed. Let's go.'

The Kid's mare wanted to run once they got clear of Oxbow, but he held her back so Baxter could keep up.

Freshly mounted, Baxter found his new horse an improvement on the one he'd ridden before, and enjoyed his first night ride as a bright moon flooded the range with silver. The grassland appeared empty of life to the distant foothills. The temperature dropped and the air turned chill.

'How are we going to find any cattle?'

'Where there's water, you'll find cows. And my horse smells water.'

Baxter realized the mare was veering to one side and increasing her pace. Then he glimpsed the river ahead, silent and gleaming. He saw animals drinking or grazing along the banks.

'Quiet now,' the Kid murmured, slowing his mare to a walk. 'Sound travels at night, and this rancher may have night guards out.'

The river curved in a wide loop with the cattle gathered in the centre; this was what had once been the Oxbow, Baxter guessed. Their horses entered the water to drink among the cows.

'Keep low in the saddle.' The Kid touched his arm and pointed.

Baxter saw, behind the herd, two night riders patrolling and crooning to their animals, and began to feel nervous. It was all right for the Kid to talk about 'running off a bunch of steers', but Hank Judson would call it rustling and rustlers got hanged. He began to sweat despite the cold.

He watched the Kid and copied his movements, drifting slowly through the shallows among the drinking cattle towards the far end of the herd away from the cowhands. He prayed for cloud to cover them but the moon stayed clear and bright.

The Kid's mare eased out of the water with hardly a splash, and he used his hat to beat the flanks of a few stragglers and turn them.

When Baxter tried it, he found the cattle reluctant to shift; obstinately, they ignored him.

He tried again, with resting animals but, when they staggered to their feet, they didn't want to leave the water's edge; they weren't used to being moved at night.

Gradually, he and the Kid got a small bunch together and moving away from the main herd, slowly heading them towards the foothills.

Hoofbeats sounded urgently behind them. The rancher's night men had spotted them and were following at a gallop. The Kid drew his revolver and fired into the ground immediately behind the slow-moving cattle and they broke into a trot.

A bullet whistled past Baxter's head as the night guards opened fire; his horse snorted and broke into a gallop. The Kid threw lead back.

After another exchange of shots, their small bunch of cattle started to run, heading for the hills. The cowhands still chased them, shooting wildly, and the cows went even faster.

In the running gunfight, the Kid closed on Baxter and hissed, 'Shoot high or low, but shoot — make them quit following us.'

Reluctantly, Baxter winged off a shot that passed over the leading rider's Stetson, but he wasn't happy. As a lawman he didn't think he should be taking someone else's cattle.

The cows were running well so the Kid slowed down and turned; he placed two careful shots, one each in the path of the following horses. They didn't like it and almost threw their riders.

The night guards gave up the chase, and the Kid and Baxter rode leisurely after the bunch they'd cut out of the main herd.

'What now?' Baxter asked breathlessly.

'There's no hurry. These cows will slow in their own time. We just trail along. Those two *hombres* have quit.'

Another hour passed before they reached the hills and the Kid used his hat to drive the cows into the mouth of a narrow canyon.

'They'll graze here a while — drag some brush across the entrance so it's not so obvious.'

The Kid got the cattle bedded down while Baxter covered their tracks.

'If the owner doesn't find them, we can sell them later, Billy.' The Kid laughed. 'I've told you before, sometimes a man is on one side of the law, and sometimes on the other.' He began to ride away.

Baxter followed. He was anxious to keep up because he suddenly realized he had no idea which way to go.

'How will we find our way back?'

'By the stars, Billy. You must study to read the constellations, then you'll never be lost at night. Leastways, not while the sky's clear.'

★   ★   ★

Carl Mueller woke from a bad dream, sweating and not sure what was happening. He'd heard the blast of a shotgun, but he'd heard that many times in his old familiar nightmare. The drumming of a horse's hoofs getting steadily louder was something new and confusing. Then he realized he wasn't dreaming that part. He was hearing a real horse approaching. He came fully awake; moonlight shining through a window into his room in the Big R ranch house showed a horseman coming at a fast clip.

He threw back the blankets and slid

into denim pants, pulled on his boots and buckled his gunbelt. He padded to the front porch.

The rider came right up to the porch and dismounted. Mueller recognized Ace Walters, one of the night guards.

'Rustlers,' the old man gasped. 'They moved out some cows, near the bend.'

His horse was lathered and trembling, with froth around its mouth. Mueller frowned. 'See to your horse first.'

Another voice came sharply from behind: Roach was up, half-dressed. 'How many rustlers?'

'I saw two. I don't know how many others there were.'

'Two!' Roach's face turned pale with fury. 'You let two men drive off my stock? I ought — '

Walters stepped backwards, mumbling. 'We chased 'em. They had a marksman who planted a couple of shots right under the noses of our cayuses.'

'Calm down,' Mueller said. 'Ace is an

old man — his partner, Oliver, is a green youngster.'

'I don't care,' the rancher snarled. 'I'll dock them a month's pay ... nobody takes anything of mine and gets away with it. We've got to get moving, Carl, catch these rustlers and hang them. Rouse the bunkhouse.'

Mueller looked up at the sky and hesitated. 'There ain't that much hurry. We don't have anybody good enough to follow tracks by moonlight. And it'll be dawn in a few hours.'

'So they'll have time to get clear away!'

'Where would they go?' The foreman turned to Walters. 'Which way were they heading?'

'Towards the hills.'

'You see, boss? They can hide in the hills — plenty of canyons up there — but where do they go after that? There's only a few ways through the hills to a possible buyer.'

Roach, still fuming, reluctantly agreed to wait till full light. 'If it's Ferris — '

'Why would Ferris run for the hills?'

The Big R rancher swore violently. 'Where's that damned sheriff? He's never around when he's wanted. Politicking, as usual, I suppose.' Roach sneered. 'Waal, this time he can do something to earn his salary. I want my cattle back!'

8

Vote Counting

Someone was shouting at the top of his voice when Billy Baxter opened his eyes. Sunlight filled the jailhouse and made him squint. It seemed he'd only just got to bed, late, when it was time to get up.

He was tempted to pull the blanket over his head, but that loud voice went on and on. What the devil was happening out there? He struggled into his clothes and tipped water from a jug into a bowl and splashed it over his face. Coffee, he thought, and headed for Stan's café.

Behind him, at the crossroads, someone was standing on the back of a buggy and talking. The annoying voice boomed and echoed and seemed to follow him. Baxter shuddered and kept going. He supposed that, as marshal, he ought to investigate, but breakfast came first.

Stan took one look at him and poured a cup of black coffee. 'Late night, Marshal?'

Baxter yawned and slumped in the nearest chair, reaching for the cup. He swallowed, drank again, and held out the cup for a refill.

'What's going on, Stan? What's that hellish row?'

'Sheriff Lamming's in town.'

'The sheriff?' Baxter sat up straighter.

Stan served him thick slices of bacon with beans and hash browns. 'Get that inside yuh. Politicking can wait.'

'Politicking?'

Baxter didn't feel very bright. Nothing seemed to make sense this morning. He supposed real rustlers slept late.

He cleared his plate, drank another cup of coffee and began to feel he might cope — until he wondered if the sheriff had somehow got on to the cows he and the Kid had stashed away in the canyon. But why should he be going on about it in public?

He went outside and moved slowly along the boardwalk. The sheriff didn't have a large audience; a few with glasses in their hands stood outside the Silver Dollar, a shopkeeper in an apron with no customers, women with children.

Baxter noticed Jerry Trumbo writing in his notebook as the sheriff began to wind down, Gus Whitney beside him. He hovered behind the cattleman, Ferris, and watched and listened.

The buggy the sheriff stood on carried a hand-painted sign: VOTE LAMMING FOR SHERIFF.

'Don't forget,' the sheriff ended, 'better a crook you know than one you don't. I've been your county lawman for more than seven years — and I never heard of a true Westerner changing horses in midstream. Why, you could end up with someone who doesn't consider your best interests! I've looked after you people of Prospect and I'll go on looking after you. All I'm asking is the chance to do just that. Remember, a vote for me is best for you!'

He doffed his Stetson with a flourish and stepped down from the buggy, a big man with sideburns wearing a loose-fitting suit. He moved with deliberation and Baxter glimpsed a shoulder holster under his coat. Baxter saw Whitney point in his direction and suddenly felt nervous under the sheriff's scrutiny; but there was no point in running. He advanced slowly to meet the county lawman.

''Morning, Colonel, 'morning, Sheriff,' he mumbled.

Lamming said, 'Are you supposed to be the Cisco Kid? I've got a reward notice with your name on it.'

'It's only a name,' Baxter said. 'I guess there must be more than one of us.' He held his breath. Lamming brought a Wanted notice from a pocket and compared the picture with Baxter's face. He nodded. 'You ain't this Kid, for sure.'

Whitney howled like a drunk deprived of his liquor. His pudgy hands clenched. 'Then he's taking money under false pretences!'

Lamming said, 'Maybe. Have you had any trouble in town since he arrived?'

'A bank robbery — '

'No marshal can protect yuh from bank robbers. I mean, is the town orderly?'

Whitney tugged at his moustache then, reluctantly, nodded.

Lamming smiled. 'Then my advice is, keep him on.'

A horseman came along First Street and Baxter saw it was Roach.

The rancher bawled, 'Lamming! There you are, at last — I've a job for you. Thieves have been running off my cattle.'

The sheriff raised an eyebrow as he recognized the hooked nose and thinning hair of the boss of the Big R. 'Your cattle? Taking a chance I'd say. Where's your foreman?'

'He's gone after them, with some of my crew.'

'Waal, if he starts hanging folk, I might have to step in.'

Roach cursed bitterly. 'I want you to track them down and hang them!'

'If I catch them,' the sheriff said calmly, 'they'll go before a judge and jury.'

Baxter's memory stirred. What was it the Kid had said? 'Irvine . . . Louis Irvine. Wanted for rustling — I've got a notice somewhere.'

'So have I,' Lamming said. 'What about it?'

'He left Oxbow recently — '

The sheriff studied him carefully. 'You're in touch with the Oxbow marshal, are you?'

'Goddamn!' Roach exclaimed, suddenly spotting Baxter. 'Here's our useless marshal, sleeping while some crook helps himself at the bank — and I had money in that bank!'

'A bad day for the Big R,' Lamming said, and nodded to the newspaper editor. 'Are you getting all this down, Jerry?'

'Sure thing, Sheriff.'

'You can quote me: 'Sheriff Lamming is hard on the heels of the robbers who held up the bank in Prospect. Likely this was one of the gang who ran off a Big R herd of cattle — ''

Another voice interrupted as Ferris pushed forward. 'It's Roach who's been stealing my cows. And the cows of other small ranchers around here. Maybe he held up the bank, too. I heard the robber rode a piebald horse and we all know — '

'You all know that piebald's a wandering horse,' Roach said. 'Anyone could have ridden it.'

Ferris persisted, 'Are you going to arrest Roach?'

Lamming shook his head. 'You're out-voted, Mr Ferris. You've got one vote — the Big R represents twenty votes at least. No contest!'

★ ★ ★

Mueller was in no hurry. The tracks of the missing cows were plain enough by daylight, and he had five armed men at his back, all cowhands with the Big R. Not in his class, but still handy with a gun if necessary.

Oliver, the green youngster who'd ridden with Ace Walters at night, was along and eager for revenge.

Mueller halted near the mouth of a canyon, studying the brush dragged across the entrance.

'Looks like a hurried job. Guess this is where — ' He paused, listening to a calf bawl. 'Oliver, clear away this brush.'

The young night guard was keen and, afterwards, they rode inside at a walking pace and in silence. Before they had gone far they saw cattle grazing; and a man at a camp-fire eating breakfast. He seemed to be alone; a stringy man with stubble on his face, who had obviously been there overnight. It was only when the Big R riders circled him that he came to his feet.

As he faced Mueller, he noted the width of the foreman's shoulders, the scowl and twin revolvers, and said, 'I ain't looking for trouble.'

'But you've found it after moving Big R cattle.'

'These? Hell, I don't know a thing about them. They were here when I arrived and decided to rest a while.'

Mueller gave a thin smile. They had the cattle; did this man matter?

'Hang him high!' That was young Oliver, who'd been one of the night guards. 'Teach this rustler not to fool with us.'

'I ain't no rustler. I'm called Bony, a bounty man — I tried for the Cisco Kid but he was too slick for me. I'm here only to keep out of his way — I've no interest in your cows.'

Mueller hesitated. He wasn't against hanging, and Roach was all for it, but he remembered the sheriff was around somewhere. The Cisco Kid?

But he didn't need trouble. He had his own plans — and he wasn't going to let anything or anyone interfere with them.

'Maybe he ain't rustling,' he said, swinging down from his saddle. He walked towards the bounty man, a revolver in his hand centred on his chest. 'But he's sure trespassing on Big R land and needs a lesson in manners. It pays to ask first.'

Bony looked around and saw other guns covering him and licked his lips. 'I figured this was open range.'

'Your mistake. Mr Roach reckons every bit of land around here is his — and I've men with me who'll swear we found you on our range. Just release your gunbelt and let it drop.'

As the bounty man hesitated, Oliver yelled, 'You're going soft, Carl!'

Bony let his gunbelt drop and stepped away.

'Now take your boots off.'

Again there was a moment's hesitation and Mueller took a step closer, eyes gleaming. 'You've one chance of getting out of this alive . . . and that's to do exactly as I say.'

Bony didn't like it but he had no choice. He sat down and tugged off one boot after the other.

Mueller climbed back on his horse. 'Get up. Now, *run*!'

He urged his mount forward and lashed the bounty man with his quirt. Bony howled, and ran. Oliver laughed and started after him, striking with his whip. Other Big R men caught on and joined the hunt, whooping loudly.

Bony had no chance of outrunning mounted men. He could only keep moving and hope they'd soon tire of the chase.

They came at him one after another and his shirt disintegrated as their whips swung and his back was criss-crossed with red weals.

'Keep running!' a Big R puncher shouted.

Their quarry needed no urging as cow ponies breathed down his neck. He had stopped cursing because he needed his breath. His socks shredded and his feet were cut by jagged stones; his back ran with blood as the hunters' quirts swung at him.

Bony blundered on, hardly aware of where he was going. Tears flooded his eyes with every stroke of leather; pain was beginning to numb his mind. He staggered and stumbled, weakening with every step. And still the riders hounded him, laughing and flailing their whips.

'Ride him down!'

Tired beyond caring he began to convulse and, finally, fell full length and lay in a bloody heap of raw flesh, sobbing.

Mueller motioned his men back. 'Enough.'

He leaned down to speak to the barely conscious and quivering victim.

'Guess you'll remember to stay off Big R range in future. When you get up, keep walking — and don't come back.'

He turned away, waving his men to collect the cows and Bony's horse, and gave young Oliver a frosty look.

'Next time you put a foot wrong, remember how soft I am.'

★ ★ ★

The Cisco Kid was amused and just a little wary. Val the Viking, as he thought of her, was magnificent and more than a little overwhelming. He was attracted, but had no intention of being hog-tied and branded.

He leaned back in his chair in the marshal's office in Oxbow, admiring her while he rolled a cigarette in slow motion.

Val was in full flood. 'Is it true,' she demanded, 'that the fake Cisco kid came here to brace you, and you talked him out of it? Some idiots are even saying you're afraid to face him in a showdown . . . but nobody seems to know what really happened. And then you rode off together. Is he still alive?'

'It's true he visited me. It's true we talked some. It's true I rode part of the way back with him.'

Her breath came faster. 'But he's — '

'Still alive, yes. Why d'you find it so strange that two lawmen — neighbours in a manner of speaking — should consult each other? We're both hired to protect honest citizens from border ruffians and their like.'

Val Neilson was looking as if she might explode when Earl limped through the doorway on his stick. Excited, he called out, 'The sheriff's here!'

'That so?' The Kid struck a match and lit his cigarette.

Val's face lost its natural colour. She muttered, 'See you later,' and hurried from the office.

The Kid stared in astonishment, then stood up and moved to the doorway. He waited, smoking and watching her. She appeared furtive as she hastened along Front Street to the livery stable; minutes later he saw her in the saddle of Rusty, riding out of town.

'Strange,' he murmured.

Earl frowned. 'Sure looks like she's

avoiding the sheriff.'

Val Neilson was quickly out of view, and the Kid turned to look the other way. A man stood on the back of a buggy carrying the slogan: VOTE LAMMING FOR SHERIFF.

His voice carried: 'It's election time again, so remember, if you don't vote me back there's no telling who you might get. You could end up with someone who wants all your saloons closed on a Sunday! Or wants a cut on what comes from your diggings. Someone not as easy-going as yours truly. Don't rock the boat. Vote for the old firm and we'll all get along as usual . . . '

Dutch Holland was scribbling in a notebook, and there was a crowd outside the Horseshoe. Dr Paul spoke to an injured miner. The atmosphere was relaxed.

Then the Kid saw Neilson come striding from his store. His face was dark as he demanded, 'Has anyone seen my daughter? Sheriff, you'll eat with us at midday. Val is supposed to be getting a meal ready, and I can't find her.'

Earl called, 'She just rode out of town, Mr Neilson.'

'Out of town?' Erik Neilson sounded astonished. 'That girl gets wilder by the day — she needs a mother's guiding hand — she knows she shouldn't be riding anywhere right now.'

The Kid finished his smoke and strolled up. The mayor asked, 'What happened to my daughter?'

'I can't figure her,' the Kid admitted. 'She just took off like a dog with a tin-can tied to its tail.'

Sheriff Lamming studied him and brought a Wanted notice from his pocket; he compared the picture with the Kid's face. 'It says here there's a reward on your head and — '

Neilson interrupted, 'Not now, Sheriff — I don't want to lose him.'

' . . . and there's the matter of a bank robbery in Prospect and — '

'Not guilty,' the Kid said cheerfully.

' . . . and Mr Roach says someone's

been running off his cattle.'

'Waal, I've been hearing stories about Mr Roach, how he takes other men's cows. Maybe somebody's just taking his own back.'

Lamming watched the Kid with a hawk's gaze. 'I also heard you're in touch with this other Kid in Prospect.'

'Two lawmen talking shop! Is that a crime now?' The Cisco Kid fashioned another cigarette and lit it. 'Why, you've probably talked to him yourself.'

He blew a smoke ring as he turned to leave.

'Remember, Sheriff, you need every vote you can get to stay in office!'

9

Gone Missing

Mueller was taking it easy in a comfortable chair when Roach got back from Prospect. The foreman was a hired gun and knew his worth; he had his feet up and a glass in his hand when Roach walked into the main room of the ranch house.

'What about my cattle?' the Big R rancher snapped.

'They're back, boss, and no harm done. They were left in a canyon. I've detailed a man to keep watch so, if the thieves return, we'll have warning. Did you find the sheriff?'

Roach poured himself a drink and swallowed it.

'I found him — with nothing on his mind except electioneering, but at least he put Ferris in his place. And that marshal in Prospect isn't the Cisco Kid after all.'

'I thought he looked too young to be the real thing.'

'The Kid's at Oxbow apparently — he's the marshal there.'

Mueller sat up and spoke sharply, 'Oxbow?'

'Why should you worry, Carl? You hardly ever visit the place.'

'I've got it in mind to go one day.' Mueller touched a gun butt. 'One day soon, maybe.'

'Waal, you can forget that for now,' Roach said. 'I've a special job for you.' He pointed through the window. 'The box strapped on my horse is for you.'

Mueller stared, then raised an eyebrow. 'That looks like — '

Roach nodded, pleased with himself. 'Dynamite, in sticks, used for blasting. I bought it at the Emporium, so nobody's likely to take much notice. Miners buy it there quite often.'

'But you're not mining — or are you?'

'Hell, no, but I've made up my mind. My cattle come first, and they'll need all the water they can get, so — '

Roach rubbed the side of his hooked nose.

'I want you to take a ride into the hills, to where the river starts to come down to the prairie. Pick your spot, set a charge and fire it. If you judge it right, the blast will block the present course of the river and divert it so the new flow reaches my land only. Clear?'

'Clear enough — but it could cause trouble. Other folk aren't going to sit on their gunhands and let you take over.'

'I can handle them. If they want water, they pay me for it. If they won't pay, I'll move them out — with force, if necessary. Is that all right with you?'

'Why not? If that's what you want . . . '

Roach filled both their glasses. 'To our very own river.'

Mueller drank slowly, thinking fast. It seemed his plans might come to a head sooner than he'd thought. He went outside, unloaded Roach's horse and loaded the wooden case on to a pack horse. He saddled a mustang and set off for the hills, smiling.

★　★　★

When Earl called out, 'The sheriff's here,' Val felt panic for the first time in her life. She stopped thinking and bolted. Like a machine in high gear she saddled Rusty, swept along Front Street and out of town away from the county lawman. It was guilt that drove her.

Once beyond the limits of Oxbow she let the stallion have his head; he liked to run.

Eventually the gears of her brain meshed again and she began to think. Where was she running to? Ahead, the hills rose on a far horizon and, as she was headed that way, the hills became her destination. There were plenty of hideouts among the hills.

She twisted around in the saddle to

look back; no one was chasing her, and she wondered why she'd bolted. Suppose the sheriff hadn't been after her? He must, by now, be puzzling over why she'd run like that. Flight implied guilt.

And her father? What must he think? They'd extended hospitality to the sheriff before . . .

She hadn't consciously assumed he was after her. The knowledge sprang to life in her head without warning; Sheriff Lamming knew, and he'd come for her.

But how could he know? It was impossible, and she'd panicked over nothing. Of course, she still had the money she'd taken from the bank, and that would be damning, if found. She'd intended to return it after a suitable interval — but right now it was still in her room above the store.

Having got clear, it seemed best to stay away; at least until the sheriff got tired of waiting for her and left town.

Val felt like having a good swear. Anyway, it was all the fault of that young idiot calling himself the Cisco

Kid. She'd only done it to show him up; to prove to the people of Prospect they had an imposter who couldn't handle the marshal's job. She'd have hit him if he'd been handy.

What would the Cisco Kid think of her, leaving him like that? Dot wouldn't be impressed either, by her running away. She felt ashamed of her weakness and was tempted to return — but she still had the money.

Suppose the sheriff arrested her? The mayor's daughter tried for theft and sent to prison . . . she shivered. Her father would be shamed and might lose his chance to be named state governor, because of her. The idea made her miserable.

Rusty was still travelling at speed towards the hills; the chestnut stallion was her only friend now.

The money was the trouble. Nobody had identified her; she'd borrowed Roach's wandering piebald and turned the animal loose afterwards. Damn that stupid imposter; she should never have let him get under her skin.

She was still trying to work out what was best to do when she became aware of another rider cutting across her path; a rider leading a pack horse and obviously not the sheriff.

She pulled on the reins to slow Rusty, not wanting to look as though she had a posse after her. Then she recognized the rider: Mueller, Roach's foreman.

* * *

Mueller was surprised when he saw Val Neilson riding alone across the prairie and apparently aiming for the hills behind Oxbow. At first he thought her horse was a runaway, but then she checked its headlong pace with the reins. He was both puzzled and pleased and rode to intercept her, slow and easy.

He had a use for Neilson's daughter and here she was, a gift. His gaze scanned the empty landscape to make sure she was alone.

As he approached, he called out, his tone respectful, 'Hi, Miss Neilson. Aren't you off your normal route?'

Her head came up sharply. 'I can ride wherever I like.'

'That's true, of course. But without an escort?'

'I can take care of myself!' She brought out a .22 revolver and held it steady on him. 'What are you doing here anyway?'

Mueller jerked a thumb to indicate the pack horse he was leading. 'A little job for the boss, up in the hills. We can ride together as you appear to be heading that way.'

'But I'm not.' She spoke abruptly, as if she didn't trust him, holstered her gun and turned her horse to ride away.

He had to think fast. If he was going to make use of her, now was the time. He had to act immediately. He took another swift look around to make sure there was nobody else in sight.

He uncoiled his lariat and made a

smooth cast. The noose settled over her shoulders and dropped, pinioning her arms. As he jerked the rope taut, his horse, a well-trained cow pony, sat on its haunches, making a solid anchor.

Rusty sailed on and Val left her saddle to hit the ground with enough force to leave her half-stunned and breathless.

Mueller hauled her in, tightening the noose, slid from the saddle and strode towards her. He took the small revolver from her and tossed it aside; maybe searchers would find it, but it wouldn't tell them much.

The chestnut returned and nuzzled her as she lay on the ground. Mueller used a spare rope to make a lead for the stallion and hitched one end to his own horse. Then he tied her hands in front of her and helped her upright.

She gulped air into her lungs. 'You must be mad! My father will kill you for this.'

'Mad? Maybe I am . . .'

He helped her back on to Rusty so

she could grip the saddlehorn, effectively a prisoner.

'What do you expect to gain by this?'

Mueller smiled but didn't answer directly. 'Behave, and I won't have to use this.' He raised his quirt and lashed her, once.

Taken by surprise, Val cried out and blinked back tears.

'You won't live to hang,' she promised fiercely. 'When I tell the Cisco Kid he'll shoot you so full of holes all your blood will drain out.'

'Then it's lucky for me you're in no position to tell anyone.'

He climbed into his saddle and started off, leading Rusty with Val aboard and the pack horse with its case of dynamite.

★   ★   ★

Neilson's store was extra busy, which kept Val's father occupied but didn't stop him worrying. She was a headstrong girl and tended to go her own way, but she wasn't one to duck work when she knew it was expected of her; and they always fed the sheriff when he visited Oxbow.

Erik Neilson was also getting hungry, and looked apologetically at Lamming.

'You can see how I'm fixed, Mr Lamming — I suggest you eat at the hotel this once.'

The sheriff nodded. 'Try to stop worrying, Mr Neilson. She's a big girl now, and well able to look out for herself.'

'I suppose she could have had a fall, but — '

'Don't start imagining things in case they happen. Wait a while to see if she turns up, or if anyone brings news of her. Give it a few hours — maybe she's just been delayed — if we hear nothing, then we'll think about organizing a search party.'

As the sheriff turned to leave, the storekeeper called, 'If you see Earl, ask him to bring me something. I can't shut the shop today.'

Lamming walked outside and along Front Street, remembering when it had been a riverfront. He spotted the lame boy and passed on Neilson's request, then continued to the hotel.

He nodded to Dutch Holland tucking into a midday meal with enthusiasm, and realized for the first time how the editor of the *Independent* had achieved his roly-poly figure.

The Kid sat alone, his back to a wall, and had already started his meal. The sheriff seated himself at his table and, over steak and potatoes, began to probe.

'I hear you're friendly with Neilson's daughter.'

'She's the one doing the chasing.'

'It happens like that sometimes, when a man has a reputation. Are you going to tell me why she took off the way she did?'

'I would if I knew, Sheriff. This is the first time I've known her to behave like this — I'm as baffled as anyone.'

'D'you reckon we should start a search?'

The Kid paused before answering, remembering how it seemed she was avoiding the law.

He studied Lamming closely. 'You don't want her for anything, do you?'

The sheriff appeared puzzled by the question. 'Of course not.'

'It's just that she seemed scared to face you when she bolted.'

'There's no reason she — '

Dutch left his table and joined them.

'If you're going looking for Val, count me in. A damn fine girl and I don't like to think something might have happened to her. I'll ride along, and I'll stick till we find her.'

★ ★ ★

Val rode in silence for a while, recovering from her fall, but she was mystified.

'Why are you doing this? When I tell Mr Roach he'll — '

Mueller gave a harsh laugh. 'I doubt I'll be seeing him again.'

126

Val took a deep breath, preparing to dig her spurs into Rusty's flanks, just to see what would happen.

Mueller was ahead of her, and drew a revolver.

'The first sign of trouble and I'll kill your horse. I don't think you want that — apart from anything else, you'd have to walk.'

Val subsided, seething, and Mueller rode on, apparently deep in thought. She was furious with herself; how could she have been so stupid?

The miles passed and the land began to climb among trees towards the source of the river. Presently, where two streams met, Mueller paused to survey the ground.

Val looked around too. Below, the prairie was deserted. Trees blocked her view of the hills, but surely there should be miners working up here somewhere?

'Get down,' he ordered and, reluctantly, she obeyed, because there was nothing else she could do.

He used another length of rope to

hobble her so she couldn't run. Then he sat on a stump of tree and wrote in pencil on an old sheet of paper he fished from his pocket. He wouldn't let her see what he'd written, but fastened it securely to Rusty's saddle and freed the horse.

'Miss Neilson, this note is for your father. Tell your horse to go home.'

She hesitated, and he picked up his quirt. With a sigh, she stroked the stallion's muzzle and whispered, 'Home, Rusty — find Dad.'

The chestnut put his head on one side and looked at her. Mueller fired a shot into the ground close to his hoofs and Rusty snorted and turned and galloped away.

She watched him go, taking her courage with him. While she'd had Rusty with her, she'd felt she'd had a friend; now she was alone with Roach's foreman.

'Dad might pay up,' she said, 'but he'll sure as hell hunt you to the ends of the earth afterwards.'

Mueller's smile had no warmth in it.

'It's not money I'm after. Start walking, in the water — and don't leave any sign. I'll be right behind with my quirt.'

'You think they won't search for me?'

'Not up here,' he said confidently.

She began to walk slowly, in water so cold it numbed her legs. Mueller followed, leading his horse and the pack horse upwards.

10

The Piebald Again

Billy Baxter had made an interesting discovery. Dot, the blacksmith's wife, squeezed a delicious lemonade that was just right for a hot dry-as-dust day. He imagined she made it for her husband, sweating over a forge and red-hot iron, but she didn't seem to mind the new marshal sitting a while with a glass.

And she was a friend of Val Neilson. He still dreamed of the Viking even if she was chasing the Kid.

He sat outside the smithy, in the shade, sipping from a glass and relaxing as he watched the world go by on Second Street. Behind him a hammer beat a tattoo as the smith shaped metal on his anvil. Dan didn't say much but appeared friendly enough.

Prospect seemed downright peaceful. Idly he watched a young man in a business suit walk towards him and recognized the bank clerk.

Arnold stopped in front of him.

'You asked me to let you know if I remembered anything else about the robbery, Marshal. At the time, I was scared and not thinking clearly — but I went slow sacking the money and picked out mostly small denomination notes and coins, so he didn't get much in total. What I think, now, is that an experienced thief would never have let me get away with that. So it was likely someone trying it for the first time.'

Baxter nodded thoughtfully. 'That makes sense, so there's no point looking for a big spender.'

After Arnold had walked on, Baxter sat brooding. Whoever it might have been was probably in the next county now.

A rider came along the street and halted outside the smithy. A cowhand dismounted, glanced at the marshal and frowned.

'We got our cows back ourselves,' he said bluntly.

'That's good — it'll save the sheriff's time.'

Baxter saw the Big R brand on the horse and a memory came back. 'You can answer a question for me — who normally rides that piebald?'

The cowhand bristled. 'Are you trying to pin the bank robbery on the Big R?'

Baxter watched him calmly. The cowboy was lanky with a single revolver on his hip; he was scowling. 'I'm accusing no one. Just asking for information.'

Dan stopped hammering and walked across to them. He stood looking at the cowhand. 'What is it, Matt? You have a problem?'

'Left hind shoe's loose.'

Dan just stood there, cramming tobacco into his pipe. He towered above the cowboy, muscles bulging.

'It's all right to answer, Matt. The

marshal ain't one to fix the blame on an innocent man.'

Matt relaxed. 'No one rides the piebald on a regular basis,' he said. 'That horse is workshy and just wanders off. Whoever grabs it — when it's around — slaps a saddle on.'

'So it could be ridden by anybody at the Big R?'

'Or anybody who finds it on the range — it's often missing. I don't believe the raider you're after is a Big R man.'

Baxter nodded. 'Thanks, Matt; you can see I had to ask.'

Dan lit his pipe and led the cowboy's horse into the smithy.

Again, Baxter thought, suspicion pointed to someone with local knowledge. Perhaps he should look for whoever was missing from their usual haunts — but the prairie extended to Oxbow on the far side of the range.

As he finished his lemonade, he recalled that the sheriff was already on his way there; and he wondered how the Kid was getting on.

* * *

The atmosphere in Oxbow was strained. Men drank more and smoked more; they stood in groups with long faces, talking in hushed voices. Val Neilson was popular and the news that she'd disappeared spread with the speed of an avalanche.

Sheriff Lamming sat in the marshal's office; unusually he wore a worried expression.

'You saw the direction she left town,' he said. 'What d'you reckon the chances of tracking her?'

'Depends if she stuck to grass,' the Kid answered. 'That chestnut of hers can sure move and I'd say has stamina too. She could have reached the hills by now and they're rocky in places. Again, she might have changed course for Prospect — she has a woman friend there.'

He sat quietly, smoking, remembering how she'd avoided the sheriff, and reluctant to get too involved with

Lamming. The sheriff gave the impression of being an easy-going politician, but the Kid had an idea that appearance might prove deceptive. He figured Lamming for a shrewd one.

A shout went up and the Kid came to his feet and stepped outside. Men were gathering around a big horse, but he couldn't see any rider.

He threw his butt on the ground and stepped on it. The sheriff, moving fast, reached the chestnut as Neilson ran from his store, calling, 'Val?'

'Empty saddle,' a bystander said. 'Rusty came back on his own.'

'I knew it!' Neilson exclaimed. 'She's had a fall. We'll organize — '

'No,' the sheriff said quickly. 'This doesn't need a crowd, I don't want her horse's tracks covered by a bunch of riders. I'll take the Kid with me, and Doc Paul. The rest of you sit tight — we'll find her. Stay with your store, Mr Neilson.'

A man ran to the doctor's house and the sheriff unhitched his horse from the buggy. Within a few minutes, the three men were riding out of town.

Neilson watched them go, vaguely feeling he ought to be with them.

Then Earl said, 'What's this?' About to lead the stallion to the livery to rub him down, he'd discovered a folded sheet of paper tucked halfway under the saddle. 'It's addressed to you, Mr Neilson.'

The storekeeper grabbed the paper and unfolded it. As he read the note, his expression changed from relief to fear and then to anger.

'The damned scoundrel! I'll take him apart, limb by limb, if he's hurt Val. I'll — '

Dutch Holland pushed forward. 'What is it, Erik?'

Neilson shoved the note at the newspaper editor, who read the pencilled scrawl quickly; and then read it aloud to the crowd:

Neilson, if you want your daughter back, withdraw your application for state recognition.

It was unsigned.

'By God,' Dutch said, 'that's black-mail! You can't give in to this.'

'Give in!' Neilson exploded, 'I'll rip his gut out and drag him to hell!'

'They'll hardly be holding her in Prospect,' someone said.

Neilson made claws with his big hands. 'Wherever Whitney's holding her, I'll choke it out of him — '

'Better let him speak first!'

'I suppose it is Whitney?' Dutch murmured.

Oxbow's mayor glared at him. 'Of course it is! Whitney and some others in Prospect — who else could it be?'

Nobody else seemed in doubt, and Dutch nodded. 'I'll ride with you.'

'And me!'

'Me too!'

The crowd scattered to get guns and horses, and soon armed and determined men rode towards Prospect to rescue Val Neilson.

★　★　★

137

Big Joe kept his shattered hand in the hill stream till ice-cold water numbed it. His feet ached from walking and he felt exhausted. He was hungry and didn't have a gun to hunt game.

He sat on a low rock and cursed the Cisco Kid. He cursed Bony, who'd run out on him.

Cursing didn't change anything but it relieved his feelings. Neither did he have money to buy food — or a drink — if he ever reached a store; the Kid had cleaned him out.

As a bounty man he'd made life miserable for those he hunted, and now he'd reached the low point in his own life. His whiskers itched and he dipped his hand in the stream and rubbed cold water over them.

He was so down the limping man was almost level with him before he recognized his previous partner. He stared blankly.

Bony had no shirt and his back was covered in dried blood. He had tied grass around his feet and used a slender branch broken from a tree to help him hobble along.

Joe smiled, forgetting his own pain. It looked as if the rat had got what he deserved. He didn't have a gun either.

'Good,' he said with enthusiasm, and Bony scowled.

'Did they leave you any money, Bony?'

'A few bucks in my pants pocket.' He unwrapped his feet and dipped them cautiously in the icy water, then lay face down.

'The Kid smashed my gunhand,' Joe volunteered.

Bony grunted. 'Some cow outfit were after rustlers and picked on me.'

'Pity they didn't hang yuh!'

Bony didn't answer for long seconds. Then he whispered, 'Quiet. D'yuh see what I see?'

Joe looked round warily. Drifting towards them, grazing, came a cowpony with irregular black and white markings.

'We've got to catch that piebald,' Bony breathed.

'Right,' Joe agreed. 'But which of us is going to ride it?'

★ ★ ★

Rusty's prints were plain enough for a time; Val Neilson seemed intent only on flight after she'd left Oxbow, which puzzled the Cisco Kid. If she wasn't fleeing the sheriff, what was going on?

Lamming still professed not to know anything, so the Kid sat easy in his saddle, just along for the ride. Some way behind them came a miner on a mule on the way to his diggings. Dr Paul remained taciturn, glancing back from time to time.

As an ex-army surgeon, he was the only man in town with more then a basic knowledge of medicine, and used to riding miles to reach a patient.

Suddenly, Lamming went up in the Kid's estimation. They were gentling along, saving their horses, when the sheriff reined back and said, 'Wait.'

He dismounted on an apparently

empty prairie to study tracks. 'She met someone here — two horses.'

He cast around and then stooped; when he straightened up he was holding a small revolver.

'That's Val's,' the Kid said. 'Now we know it wasn't a fall. Something happened to her.'

'*Someone* happened to her,' Lamming corrected.

Dr Paul had lingered to talk to the miner, who had caught up with them. He called, 'Another complication, Sheriff.'

Lamming and the Kid turned to the miner, a burly man with grey in his beard.

'Sheriff, they found a note on Miss Neilson's horse. It demanded the mayor quit trying for Oxbow as state capital — he figured Whitney's behind it.'

The miner's expression was serious.

'Mayor Neilson was real upset and shouting loud enough to scare crows. He's getting a whole lot of Oxbow men to storm Prospect and get her back.'

Lamming swore. 'The damn fool! He won't learn anything by starting a war, just get a lot of heads broken for nothing.'

'So where's my patient?' the doctor asked.

Lamming and the Kid looked at each other, and the Kid said, 'We've got to find Val.'

'And I've got a war to stop,' the sheriff countered. 'I want you with me, Kid, and you too, Doc. We'll likely need more than one bone-mender to patch holes and set limbs when they start swinging at each other.'

'I figure Miss Neilson will be all right for now — she's a pawn in this game and no use dead.' He looked grim. 'I never thought Gus had much brain, but this is downright stupid . . . if it is him. Grabbing a woman to use as hostage is likely to lead to all hell breaking loose.'

He spoke to the miner. 'I want you to tell anyone you see in the hills to keep a lookout for her.'

'Surely will.'

'C'mon.' Sheriff Lamming rode towards Prospect, with Doctor Paul and the Kid following. But now he increased the pace.

11

Riot

Baxter had moved a chair from his office on to the boardwalk so he could sit outside. Second Street was quiet and he was deliberating whether or not to visit Stan for coffee and a chat; definitely not a meal.

Stan's meals were sized for men who did active work, and the marshal was putting on weight where he didn't need it; unlike Hank Judson, who remained as fit as an athlete no matter what happened to him.

Baxter found himself slowing down and short of breath after any little extra effort. His life of adventure seemed to have slid into an easy-going routine.

That was before he heard urgent hoofbeats on First Street. A thunderous drumming sounded like a whole bunch of riders coming at a gallop. He saw horses milling around at the crossroads and men with guns in their hands.

He came out of his chair as a voice bellowed, 'Where's Whitney? Come out of hiding, you yellow cur — we're here for an accounting.'

Baxter quickened his stride. The riders, unknown to him, had grim expressions. 'What's going on?' he asked.

A horseman swung a revolver to cover him. 'If you've any sense, Marshal, you'll stay out of this. We're here on serious business.'

The batwing doors of the Silver Dollar swung open and Colonel Gus Whitney stepped out, glass in hand.

'Who — ? It's you, Neilson!' The Mayor of Prospect looked around him and recognized some of the men from Oxbow. 'What the devil is all this about?'

Erik Neilson climbed down from his saddle, balled a massive hand and swung. Whitney was late in dodging and, though the fist barely grazed him, was knocked flying. He landed on his back in the dust and chose to stay down. Neilson bawled, 'Get up, you dog! Get up and I'll kill you!' He aimed a kick to encourage Prospect's mayor.

Neilson was large and heavy; Whitney plump and out of condition. If Neilson wasn't stopped it would be murder.

Baxter pushed through the crowd and grasped Neilson's arm. 'No more — '

Neilson brushed him aside as he would an insect.

'Have you gone mad, Erik?' Whitney asked from the ground.

Other riders dismounted and hauled the mayor to his feet. One jabbed a revolver in his side. Another shouted, 'Get a rope — string him up!'

But Neilson didn't need a gun or a rope. His hands curled around Whitney's throat, choking off the air from his lungs.

He lifted him off his feet and shook him, yelling at the top of his voice as if

Whitney were deaf: 'Where's my daughter, damn you? What have you done with her? Speak up or I'll break you in two!'

Baxter was startled; this was the first he'd heard of anything happening to Val.

Dutch Holland tried to break Neilson's stranglehold. 'No, Erik . . . if you throttle him, he won't be able to tell us where she is.'

Neilson shifted his grip so Whitney could breathe again. Gus gulped air and said hoarsely, 'I don't know anything about your daughter. I haven't — '

Neilson hit him again as men came running from the Silver Dollar and the hotel, pulling guns.

'Leave Gus alone, you damn bully! What the hell's going on here?'

'It's a bunch of Oxbow men — send 'em back where they came from!'

Jerry Trumbo flourished his notebook under the note of the *Independent*'s editor. 'Quick, Dutch, what's this about? Give me the story.'

Dan the blacksmith arrived. 'Looks like you need a little help, Marshal. What's this about Val, Mr Neilson?'

'She's missing! Went riding and never got back . . . they sent a note by her horse.'

He flourished a piece of paper. 'This tells me to quit running Oxbow for state capital . . . obviously only Whitney's low-down bunch of crooks would pull a dirty trick like that.'

'You've no evidence,' Baxter said quickly, 'and I don't believe it.' He had his gun out now. 'I've an interest in Val, too.'

Dan said loudly, 'No one here would hurt Val, Mr Neilson — she's a friend of my wife's. Calm down.'

'Of course I wouldn't harm her,' Whitney said, getting his courage back. 'It's all a mistake.'

The mayor of Oxbow roared, 'It's not a mistake — Rusty returned alone!'

A voice at the back of the crowd chanted, 'Drive these Oxbow idiots out!'

'Quiet down,' Baxter said, 'or I'll throw you in jail.'

Another voice called, 'Let's use Whitney for target practice!' A revolver fired. 'The hell with Prospect — burn the place to the ground!'

★　★　★

The piebald horse ignored the two bounty men beside the stream. It grazed its way slowly closer to the water, then dipped its head to drink. Joe and Bony tensed, eager to make a grab.

Joe was quickest despite his weight and, one-handed, hauled himself on to the animal's back.

'Me!' he exclaimed triumphantly. 'I'm the one who gets to ride — that'll teach yuh to run out on me.'

He dug his heels into the horse's flanks, sending it uphill and leaving Bony to hobble after on his stick.

'You rat,' the stringy man yelled, scowling; if he'd had a gun he'd have used it.

Joe ignored him, disappearing around a bend in the trail, laughing.

Bony felt murderous. It had been a mistake to partner Joe in a try for the bounty on the Cisco Kid. The whole idea had been a mistake, and he promised himself he'd never again take a partner.

He limped back to the river and continued soaking his feet. He damned Joe thoroughly, and hoped the horse's owner caught up with him.

He was just beginning to relax when he heard the faint sound of horses splashing through water. Before he saw anyone he crawled back and crouched behind a rock. He wanted to see who it was before revealing himself. Unable to move quickly and unarmed, he was wary of anyone walking horses that way.

He glimpsed one rider and a pack horse; and a woman walking with her hands tied.

Bony flattened himself to the ground, hardly breathing; he didn't want this rider to see him. A man who took a woman prisoner would be dangerous. He was puzzled, because any man who treated a woman that way was asking for trouble.

He studied the rider as he passed; a two-gun *hombre* with long, dark hair and broad shoulders. Bony recognized him; it was the man who'd whipped him, the foreman leading the Big R cowhands.

Hatred bubbled like champagne in his veins, taking Bony to the point of recklessness. His sudden need for revenge was so overwhelming that he almost flung himself at the rider, and barely restrained himself in time. He would have been dead before he reached the bastard.

For the moment he could only hide, and follow. After they passed, Bony carefully rewrapped his feet and took up his stick. The woman was obviously tired and couldn't hurry.

He settled to a steady pace, ignoring his pain. He had the best salve in the world: a burning desire for vengeance.

'Burn the place to the ground!'

Sheriff Lamming's blood froze as he rode into Prospect with the Cisco Kid and Dr Paul. A riot in town was something all lawmen feared.

As a revolver fired, he drew his shotgun and checked the loads.

It was obvious Gus Whitney was at the centre of the trouble. The blacksmith and Baxter were trying to pull Neilson off him, but the Oxbow mayor was like a wild man, screaming, 'I want my daughter back!'

Around them milled a crowd of men of Prospect and Oxbow grappling hand-to-hand. The two rival editors were getting it all down in their notebooks. A voice bawled, 'Swing him high,' and another, 'Shoot 'em if they won't get out of town!'

Lamming didn't waste his voice; he raised his shotgun, pointed the barrels over the heads of the mob and pulled both triggers. Shot fell like hail over the combatants while the sheriff broke his gun and thumbed in two more shells.

'The next loads won't be over your heads. This is the law — break it up and quieten down.'

In the pause in the battle, the Kid rode his mare in among the crowd, laying about with his revolver barrel so men of both factions dropped.

Eventually Lamming and the Kid calmed the over-excited mob.

'Now,' the sheriff said, 'we'll talk sense instead of hot air.' He held out the small revolver he'd found. 'Can you identify this, Mr Neilson?'

'Yes, it's hers — Val's — sure enough. Where did you get it?'

'On open range, halfway to the hills.'

Neilson was silent, mystified.

'Let me see the note.'

Neilson handed it to Lamming, who read it and showed it to Whitney. 'Did you write this, Gus?'

'Of course I didn't,' the Mayor of Prospect snapped. 'As if I'd hurt a hair of Val's head.'

The sheriff showed the note around, but nobody recognized the writing. 'Has anyone seen Miss Neilson today? Does anyone have an idea where she might be?'

There was silence, while Dr Paul and the Prospect physician attended to the injured.

Lamming read the note aloud. 'Does anybody know anything at all about this? You can see why Mr Neilson jumped to the wrong conclusion. I figure someone calculated he'd do just that — the note was a trick to throw us on the wrong track.'

The Big R rancher stepped from the bank doorway, where he'd been watching with some amusement. He pushed forward. 'Let me see that. I hadn't realized something had happened to Miss Neilson.'

Lamming showed him the note. 'Recognize anything about it?'

Roach hesitated, reading it again. He rubbed the side of his big nose, frowning, and spoke slowly.

'It's ridiculous, of course, but it looks like my foreman's hand. He doesn't often leave a written message for me, so I can't be sure . . . but why would he do this?'

Baxter thought: Roach's hired gun? He worried for Val. 'Isn't it unusual for you to be in town without him? Exactly where is Mueller right this minute?'

* * *

Val Neilson was fed up with walking. She had the normal appetite of a healthy young woman and she was hungry. Her legs had lost all feeling as she struggled uphill through icy water.

'Wait,' she snapped, jerking on the rope. Mueller paused briefly, and she stooped to cup her hands to scoop up water. She intended to drink whenever she could if he intended to starve her into submission.

He pulled on the rope impatiently and she moved on again, wondering at his purpose. He'd said he wasn't after ransom money, but could she believe that? So far he hadn't touched her.

She wished she'd been able to see what he'd written in the message Rusty had carried back. Obviously her father would be looking for her. And the Kid? Of course he was, she decided, and hoped it would worry her captor.

'The Cisco Kid will hunt you down,' she told him. 'I sure wouldn't want to be in your boots when he catches up.'

Mueller sneered. 'He might scare Roach — he doesn't scare me.'

'I don't mean that imposter at Prospect. I mean the *real* one at Oxbow. I'd like to see you face him.'

Mueller grunted. 'I remember — Roach mentioned him. It doesn't matter now.'

They continued uphill, between trees; from time to time Mueller paused to survey the land. What was he looking for? Surely he didn't intend to dig for gold? Apparently he didn't care whether she lived or died, so why was he dragging her along? She calculated her chances of escape.

He carried two revolvers in waist holsters, and she'd heard he was fast with them; but there must be miners around somewhere in these hills.

In a scabbard on his horse he had a Winchester rifle. Now, if she could get her hands on that . . .

12

Scream in the Night

Roach hesitated before answering Baxter's question.

'If it concerns you, Mueller's up in the hills — prospecting.'

From the boardwalk, a storeman from the Emporium called, 'That's right, Sheriff. Mr Roach bought a case of dynamite just recently.'

The Big R rancher turned and walked away, and Baxter would have sworn he was smiling. Dynamite? He'd heard that Roach was interested in Val.

Behind him, men drifted towards a saloon, or the hotel. The fight had ended, and still nobody knew where Val Neilson was.

Lamming tapped him on the shoulder. 'Can I borrow your office, Marshal?'

Baxter nodded absently, and the sheriff and both mayors walked off to discuss the situation in private.

Baxter was still staring after Roach when Ferris came up to him. The stumpy cattleman who'd once accused Roach of stealing his cattle was frowning.

'D'yuh believe him? In the hills maybe — but prospecting?'

'What else would he use dynamite for?'

'When you figure it out, Marshal, come and talk to me.'

Baxter wasn't interested. He was puzzled by Val's disappearance, and worried for her. He called out to the Kid, 'Have you any idea where Val is?'

The Kid shook his head, moved closer and lowered his voice. 'She took off when the sheriff arrived — I don't know why — and all we've found so far is her revolver.'

'And Mueller is somewhere in the hills,' Baxter said. 'I'm going after her. Will you come with me? I don't trust

Mueller — or Roach.'

'Why not?' the Kid drawled. 'I'd purely love to know why the law scared her like that.' He studied the sky. 'But we won't get far today. It'll be dark soon, and we'll have to wait for morning to find her tracks.'

Billy Baxter hurried to the livery to saddle his horse. He didn't like to think of Val Neilson alone in the open at night . . . or worse, not alone.

★　★　★

It was already growing dark and Val was tired and hungry. She'd never walked so far before and the muscles in her legs ached. Surely Mueller would have to stop soon?

She was beginning to hate the man. Being dragged along at the end of a rope like an animal hurt her pride, and she had fantasies about what she'd do to him as soon as she got her hands free.

At last he left the stream and

160

threaded a way between shadowy trees to a sheltered place. He turned both horses loose to graze, but didn't light a fire.

He hitched the free end of rope securing her to the branch of a tree; at least it was long enough for her to sink to the ground and rest her back against the trunk.

He sat on a broken-off branch, silently watching her, his face a mask that revealed nothing. Presently he opened a bag and brought out cold meat and bread and began to eat. He washed it down with water from his canteen.

She didn't want to ask him for anything, but she was starving. 'I'm hungry,' she said.

His smile was thin. 'Reckon you ain't going to need anything.'

He put his canteen away and tightened the drawstrings on his bag. He stood up and shook out a blanket.

Apprehensive, she wondered what he intended. But he only stretched out in a hollow, the blanket around him and his saddle for a pillow.

He said in a conversational tone, 'If you make a sound in the night it'll be the worse for you . . . and don't think I'll fall for a woman's trick of offering your body. I've got something quite different in mind for you.'

He lay back and closed his eyes.

Val felt an icy chill run down her spine. Her situation seemed even more frightening. She tried to curl into a ball as the shadowy trees merged into a wall of darkness surrounding her, but she doubted if she'd be able to sleep.

★   ★   ★

Bony had dropped behind. His feet were hurting and he doubted he could go on much longer. Was the bastard never going to make camp? Already the sun was sinking, the shadows lengthening.

Still he followed the stream upward,

hoping they hadn't turned off somewhere. The light was getting too weak to read sign; soon it would be dark. He paused, listening, but heard nothing beyond a breeze stirring the leaves.

He began to shiver as the temperature dropped; his stomach rumbled. Damn! They must have left the water, he decided, but there was no glimmer of a camp-fire. The shadows between the trees grew darker.

He had to face the fact; he'd lost them. But only for the moment. He'd wait for dawn to reach the hills and then search for tracks.

He cupped his hands to drink and then climbed the bank and dried his legs with leaves. He found a hollow and burrowed down. After a while, he dozed, thinking of the man who'd whipped him.

Sometime in the night, he woke briefly when a dreadful scream punctured the stillness, and felt envious. The lucky bastard had a woman to keep him warm . . .

Val moved restlessly. She was cold and couldn't get comfortable on granite-hard ground. Moonlight peeked through the leaves to reveal shifting shadows; then cloud drifted across the sky and the night became black as a tar pit.

Mueller was somewhere behind her, a huddled shape that jerked spasmodically and muttered in his sleep.

She supposed she must have dozed, but hunger was turning this into the longest night of her life. She gnawed at the ropes binding her. She picked at the knots but only broke her nails; if there was one thing Mueller was good at it was tying knots. Her hands were numb and she worked without feeling.

A breeze stirred and she felt a wave of chilled air break over her. A small animal scuttled by, pausing to sniff at her. She must have dozed again . . .

She woke with a start. Something

was screaming; the most terrifying sound she'd ever heard. Her heart stopped for a moment; then she jerked upright, trying to see into the shadows.

A predator seizing its prey? The screaming changed to a wailing, then a moaning. She heard Mueller stir and climb to his feet.

Moonlight was bright, showing his pale face and shaking hands. A nightmare, she supposed, startled; he'd not seemed a man with any nerves at all.

He stumbled towards her, his expression vicious. It obviously pleased him that she was tied and helpless. He kicked her, muttering, 'Bitch!'

She tried to edge away, but the rope restrained her, and he kept kicking her. Watching his face she was scared for her life; he seemed hardly to know what he was doing.

Suddenly the sky lightened, the horizon tinged with red, and he made an effort to regain control. He stared down at her, murmuring, 'Not long

. . . not long now till my nightmare ends.'

He smiled, a cat playing with an injured bird, and he added one more word, almost too low for her to hear:

'*Bait!*'

★ ★ ★

Baxter fretted because the Kid wouldn't hurry as they crossed the prairie towards the hills. The Kid pointed out where they'd found Val's revolver, and she'd met a rider leading a pack horse.

He concentrated on tracking Rusty before the light failed. As they started uphill, the Kid slid out of the saddle and began to walk, leading his mare.

Baxter said, irritated, 'We're losing time.'

'Perhaps. But if you save your horse now, she might save your life later on.'

Baxter dismounted reluctantly and started to walk. After a time, the hill seemed to get steeper and his calves hurt. A bit further and he was panting, his face red. His lungs felt as if they were going to burst.

The Kid climbed on relentlessly. 'You've let yourself get out of condition, Billy.'

Baxter didn't answer; he needed all his breath. It was never like this for Hank Judson, he reflected; when the fighting marshal rode to the rescue it was at a gallop.

He kept going, getting further behind, and was glad to stop when the Kid said it was too dark to see any tracks.

13

Threat from the Past

Carl Mueller was feeling pleased with himself. The morning air was warm and clear and his luck was in. He knew it was going to be a good day; perhaps *the* day . . .

He'd been climbing since dawn and now he'd found what he needed; a point where two streams met, blocked by an accumulation of boulders, fallen trees and other debris. An ideal place to set an explosive charge; a lot of water had piled up behind this natural dam, just waiting for release.

He was no longer concerned with Roach's plan; the Big R didn't mean a thing to him now he had Neilson's daughter in his hands; and the note he'd sent to Oxbow would give him time to complete his trap without interference.

Thinking of the idiots chasing over to Prospect made him smile. He had time to take care and be thorough. He wanted no slip-up at the last minute because he might get only the one chance before the law caught up.

He imagined the explosion, the dam collapsing and the huge volume of water released in a torrent, sweeping everything before it as it poured downhill — a flood, a deluge — an avalanche of water that would bury the trees directly in its path.

He smiled: perfect.

Then, from the corner of his eye, he caught a glimpse of Val Neilson stealthily edging towards his horse. His smile disappeared as she reached for the Winchester in its scabbard next to the saddle. Even with her hands tied, she started to draw it out.

He moved fast. A few long strides and he closed with her, his hand pulling a revolver with lightning speed. He slammed the barrel down on her right wrist and she cried out and dropped the rifle. He picked it up and checked it, replaced it in the scabbard.

Scowling, he jerked her away from the horse. His anger was mounting; she could have ruined everything. He holstered his revolver, breathing hard.

'Bitch!' He hit her across the mouth with the back of his hand. 'Stupid cow!'

She staggered and spat blood.

'A real tough gunman . . . has to tie a woman before he can hit her. You'd better start running before I get free!'

'Free?' His laugh was mocking. He took a coil of rope from behind his saddle and pushed her before him, downhill.

Val felt bewildered. First he'd forced her to climb up; now he pushed her back down. 'What's this in aid of? Why are you doing this?'

She stumbled on the uneven ground, lurching from tree to tree, until he hauled her to a standstill. As she leaned against a tree-trunk for support, he began to lash her to the trunk, facing uphill. He made sure there was no chance of her wriggling free, drawing the ropes cruelly tight and testing each knot to make it secure.

'Are you mad?' she asked, but he didn't answer immediately. Instead, he made a pad of an old glove, forced it into her mouth and tied it in place with his bandanna; he took particular care she could still breathe. He didn't want her choking to death before he was ready.

When he'd finished, he brought his face close to hers.

'What's it all about? It means I've got you where I want you and nobody knows exactly where. It means your father will worry himself sick and run around in circles like a headless chicken. He'll start to believe you're dead, but he won't be sure. He'll go on searching, losing hope . . .'

Val stared back, appalled; his face had twisted into a mask of hatred. She'd never guessed such hate could exist in anyone. His lips drooled — he was losing control again — and his eyes burned like those of a fanatic. His words frightened her.

'When Neilson finally gets up here I'll blow the dam up top to bury you under a flood right in front of him. He'll see everything and be too late to save you. Then I'll centre my rifle and kill him. Now you *know*!'

★   ★   ★

Lamming rode alongside Erik Neilson on the way back to Oxbow. The meeting had achieved nothing, and he approved of the two marshals taking off for the hills to search for Val Neilson.

It was now obvious that putting the blame on Gus Whitney had been a delaying tactic. Whoever had seized Neilson's daughter had gained the advantage of time; it was not yet clear why this was necessary.

Gus knew nothing, that was certain; the sheriff wasn't so sure about

Neilson. The Oxbow storekeeper puzzled him.

In the evening light, he no longer appeared a big, outgoing man; it seemed the heart had been taken from him. His face had an unhealthy grey colour and he seemed to have both aged and shrunk. The previously tough Swede rode slumped in the saddle.

Lamming said quietly, 'Is there anything you want to tell me, Erik?'

For a moment Neilson rode on, ignoring the question. Then he sighed and shook his head.

Lamming didn't push it; he'd learnt patience. He was worried about Neilson and thought he might ask Dr Paul to keep an eye on him. This was more than a missing daughter and, eventually, Neilson would need to talk about it.

* * *

Baxter was up early and eager to get moving. The Cisco Kid picked up the trail and followed it to the point where Rusty had been sent back and Val entered the stream.

'What now?' Baxter asked. 'If only you'd carried on when you found her gun. She could be in real trouble.'

The Kid smiled. 'Life is just one 'if only' after another, Billy. I reckon she went upstream.'

They followed the stream until the Kid paused to study fresh tracks beside the water. 'Looks like someone on foot, using a stick — whoever it is also appears to be travelling the same route.'

'Assuming Mueller has her, d'yuh reckon this is Roach's idea?'

'I doubt that. I'm beginning to think Mueller and Roach have parted company — at least, that's my guess.'

They continued between the trees, following the stream upward. The Kid slowed after a while, murmuring, 'We don't want to overtake them till we see what the situation is.'

Baxter was about to argue the point when he saw a thin figure sitting on the bank ahead of them. His feet were wrapped in grass and he'd been using a stick to help him along. The sitting man looked back and waited for them.

As they neared, he drawled, 'Waal, two marshals . . . guess you ain't chasing me.'

Baxter began, 'No, we're — '

Something about the stringy man's silhouette alerted the Kid, and he interrupted. 'You wouldn't be a bounty man, by any chance?'

'I might have been once . . . but I sure ain't interested now.' He turned to show his back. 'I owe this *hombre* I'm following — either of you a gun to spare?'

Baxter shuddered. 'Mueller did that?'

'If that's his name? Ramrodding a cow outfit — long dark hair and two guns.'

'It is Mueller!' Baxter said.

'My name's Bony. You marshals looking for a missing woman?'

'Yes,' Baxter said eagerly. 'Have you seen her? Is she all right?'

'Still alive the last I saw of her. Heard her screaming and he knocked her about a bit.'

'This Mueller,' the Kid said. 'Got a pack horse, right?'

'Yeah, with a case lashed to the horse.'

The Kid nodded. 'Figures. Heard he's got dynamite in that case.'

'That so?' It didn't register with Bony. 'I just want to lay hands on him.'

'Where is she?' Baxter demanded.

Bony gave a crafty grin. 'I'll tell yuh, Marshal, if you give me your gun.'

Baxter didn't hesitate. He gave Bony his revolver and the bounty man checked the load and shoved it in his belt.

'Strange thing,' he said. 'He took her up top, then brought her down again. Tied her to a tree' — he pointed — 'in there somewhere. He went on up again. Sure can't figure what he thinks he's doing.'

'I'm going after Mueller,' the Kid said, and continued uphill with Bony.

Billy Baxter headed eagerly in among the trees to find Val Neilson.

* * *

Val shivered. Mueller's sanity had been consumed by hatred and, for the first time in her life, she was frightened of a man.

She had no doubt he was mad; his eyes glowed as a terrible accusation spewed from his lips.

'Your father murdered my young brother Peter. They were supposed to be partners and he killed him in cold blood. Partners on a claim they dug together for gold . . .'

His stubbled face almost touched hers as he shouted, 'Everything was fine till they made a strike, and then Neilson murdered him — emptied a shotgun into his belly and left him to die alone and in agony . . .'

She would have denied every word if the gag hadn't silenced her. My father isn't like that, she screamed silently, he's a loving, caring man.

'Your father cleaned out the claim, taking all the gold there was, and rode away. Peter was still alive when he left!'

Spittle splashed her face as he yelled, 'Our parents had died and there was just Peter and me. I was working on a ranch when I heard and I swore I'd make your father pay. That time has come; not just to kill him, to make him sweat, make him worry over *his* family, make him sorry he double-crossed my brother.'

Mueller raised his quirt and struck her.

'Now d'you understand? I want him to suffer. I want to hurt him before I kill him!

'I've been hunting ever since until I found him. I've waited for the right moment, savouring the taste of revenge, waiting for you to be delivered into my hands.'

She struggled to free herself, without success.

'He'll see you die . . . before I shoot him!'

Mueller hissed the final words and struck her again. Then his mind seemed to wander, as if he'd lost the thread of his thoughts and he shook uncontrollably.

He turned away, his eyes strangely blank; he might have forgotten she existed. Without a word, without looking back, he walked up the trail.

Val Neilson felt tears leak down her cheeks. Could her father really be the monster Mueller claimed? The idea paralysed her. It was unthinkable; there had to be a mistake.

She'd always admired her father and looked up to him; now she was badly shaken and unsure and trying hard not to believe. If only she hadn't robbed the bank!

14

Deluge

Mueller felt like the calm at the centre of a hurricane. The years of waiting were coming to an end. He had baited the trap and any time the animal could walk into it; that's how he thought of Erik Neilson, an animal.

He shook back his hair so he could see what he was doing. The case of dynamite lay open on the ground beside him as, one by one, he carefully placed each stick and ran a length of fuse joining them to get one huge explosion.

He was happy in his work, happier than he'd been for a long time; this was the culmination of studying Neilson from a distance, deciding how best to hurt him, planning to get the daughter on her own.

'Soon, Peter, soon,' he murmured.

He calculated where best to place his explosive to get the result he wanted: a deluge like a huge wave rushing headlong for the trees lower down the hillside.

He'd picked a weak point in the dam so the water would burst through with maximum force; flooding Big R land was no longer a concern of his.

From time to time, he paused and stood up to survey the surrounding land, watching for Neilson to come into view.

He'd made only a token effort to hide his tracks; anyone used to reading sign would have little difficulty. He wanted his brother's murderer to follow and watch, unable to help as his daughter drowned.

He had the dynamite in place, the fuses ready for a match. He settled to wait and watch.

Presently he heard sounds from below, picked up his rifle and took cover. He needed to see but not be seen; at least, not till he had the man he hated in his sights. Then, at the last moment, he would declare his identity.

He saw two figures toiling slowly up the hillside, and frowned. Neither was big enough to be Neilson. One rode a horse, the other walked with a stick. He could guess the identity of the walker, but who was it on the horse?

In any case, they had to be discouraged. No matter who they were, he didn't want them around to confuse the issue.

He drew a bead on the horseman, squeezed the trigger and the rider was knocked sideways from the saddle. He didn't get up, and the walking man dived for cover as the horse swung about and ran downhill.

Where the hell was Neilson? Hadn't he got back from Prospect yet? Was he too cowardly to show himself? Or didn't he care about his daughter? Doubt began to edge into his mind.

He'd been so sure the big Swede would come charging after his daughter without stopping to think, straight into the trap set for him. He felt frustrated and angry because Neilson wasn't behaving as expected.

He was impatient for revenge. He'd waited long enough and, as he crouched over the fuse, his hand holding the match began to twitch. He waited to strike it . . .

★   ★   ★

Val Neilson had never felt so alone, so desperate, not even when her mother died. That was a bad time, but her father had been there to comfort her, and Dot . . .

Dot would call her an idiot for getting herself into this situation. And her father, if he found where she was, would only trigger the trap.

Mueller scared her because she'd never had to cope with a mad person before.

And just when she'd found the man she wanted to share her life . . . where was the Kid? What was he doing? Why didn't he come for her?

All feeling was gradually leaving her body where the ropes stopped the flow of blood. She couldn't call out to warn anybody because of the gag. She wasn't thinking too clearly, just remembering . . .

How big the store had seemed when she was small . . . its fascinating smells, coffee and leather and molasses and . . .

She recalled her own room, the hut that served as a schoolroom . . . and Rusty.

Her head came up as she thought about the chestnut stallion. Someone must have found him by now and wondered what had happened to her. Perhaps the Kid was following Rusty's tracks? But Mueller would be watching for her father.

She resigned herself to waiting for the end with fading hope, sad that life which had promised so much was about to be cut short.

Suddenly, through the trees, she

heard a single shot. Had Mueller fired at somebody? Had somebody shot him?

Her heartbeat quickened and blood flowed again. If only she weren't gagged she could have shouted for help — it might be a hunter.

Deliverance could be one shout away but she couldn't let whoever it was know she was here. She could have cried with frustration . . . furious with that idiot in Prospect who was the cause of all this.

* * *

The Cisco Kid lay still as a rock in the brush beside the stream, scarcely breathing. For the moment the hillside was quiet and he waited, hoping that Mueller would ignore him under the impression he was the limping and unarmed bounty man.

He could afford a small smile. His offer to let Bony ride his horse to ease his sore feet had been calculated; he hadn't forgotten the stringy man had tried to gun him down in Oxbow.

So Bony rode in his saddle and became a target, and the Kid learnt to respect Mueller's marksmanship. One shot was all it had taken and Bony had collected his last bounty.

The Kid wondered what Mueller was doing up top, but preferred not to find out the hard way. He remained motionless, not even trying to roll a smoke. Time passed slowly. How far had his horse run before stopping? Had Billy found Val Neilson yet?

The sun was hot and he watched an insect shift its position under a bush to keep in the shade. He strained his ears to catch any sound —

The explosion temporarily deafened him. He saw water rise into the air to form a giant wave that went crashing down the hill — luckily not the side where he lay.

The Kid did not often admit he could feel fear, but now he was frightened. It was as if a river stood on end and fell over. It carried small trees and bushes before it, the way an avalanche does . . . and he remembered Bony had said Neilson's daughter was tied to a tree down there.

He could do nothing except hope Billy was in time.

He studied the crest of the hill, but neither saw nor heard Mueller. He whistled for his mare and, after a while, she came up the hill. The Kid collected Baxter's revolver and rode on up.

Mueller had gone and water covered his tracks.

Baxter pushed his horse between the trees on the hillside, searching for Val Neilson. He'd given his revolver to Bony but still had his hunting knife. He called her name but there was no answer. Tied to a tree, he'd said, but there were a lot of trees.

Behind him the crack of a rifle shot sounded and he looked back; both the Kid and Bony were out of sight.

He pressed on and the moment he saw her, his heart lifted; a shaft of sunlight turned her fair hair to gold.

Then he saw she was gagged as well as tied and began to hate Mueller: he felt a fury build up inside him. He shouted, 'I'm coming, Val!'

Her head lifted and her eyes registered his approach; she was alive . . .

But before he reached her a violent explosion sounded higher up the hill. Startled, he glanced up. Why would anyone . . . ?

Appalled, he saw a massive wall of water rushing down at them and realized it was going to bury her.

He spurred his horse savagely so it charged towards her and hurled himself from the saddle as the animal was swept from under him and carried away down the hill.

The water was cold as ice and spray got up his nose and into his eyes, blinding him. He reached out to grab one of the ropes holding her and hauled himself in front of her.

He used his body to shield her from the worst of the deluge, hanging on with one hand while he used his knife

188

to cut away the gag so she had a better chance to breathe. As soon as the bandanna fell away, she spat out a wad of cloth.

For seconds that seemed like long minutes he could only cling to the ropes binding her to the tree as water rushed over and around them and they concentrated on getting air into their lungs. They were submerged beneath a torrent as if floodgates had opened, trying to breathe underwater. If they had been back in San Francisco, Baxter would have likened this to a tidal wave.

After a while the worst was over and the level of water began to drop. Waves still showered him and a broken branch threatened to sweep him away. Still gasping for breath Baxter started to saw at the ropes with his knife. He worked slowly because his hands were frozen — and partly because the ropes had cut off her circulation.

She could never have resisted the tug of water still pouring down the hill. It was not until the level sank around their ankles that he finally freed her and helped her stand.

She tried to smile as she croaked, 'Thanks.'

They stood staring at each other, drenched and shivering, until she burst into tears.

As he put his arms around her, she murmured, 'And after all the dreadful things I said about you — you really must be the Cisco Kid!'

15

Return of the River

Earl limped into Neilson's store, shouting his excitement. 'It's coming . . . it's back . . . come and see!'

Sheriff Lamming had been trying to persuade the storekeeper to talk and not getting anywhere. He was irritable.

'What is it, Earl?'

'The river — the water's rising!'

Lamming turned and strode to the door and looked out on Front Street. He frowned at a gathering crowd, and saw Dutch Holland with his notebook; the newspaperman was as excited as the lame boy.

'We're going to have a waterfront again!'

Where before there had been a mud flat, Lamming now saw rising brown water.

'We lost our river when it changed course,' Dutch said. 'Now it's changed again and we'll get our Oxbow back.'

Lamming turned to the storekeeper, who had followed him outside. 'D'you see that, Erik? Something's affected the river's course — something up there.' He shifted his gaze to the distant hills.

Neilson's expression remained sour. 'Does it matter? Does anything matter? Where's my daughter?'

Dr Paul joined them.

'You should try to relax, Mr Neilson. Two good men are following her tracks, and they'll find her in the end. And this is something that's happened up in the hills.'

'There has to be a connection,' Lamming said.

The doctor had insisted Neilson keep working; the sheriff had discouraged a posse riding out.

As the water rose higher, more people gathered to watch and wonder, but Neilson's anguish did not lift. The saloons emptied and men laid bets how high the water would rise.

Suddenly a shout went up and heads turned. Two horses were coming along the street. One horse carried two riders, and one of those was Val Neilson.

Dutch Holland was the first to reach her. 'Miss Neilson, please, a quick word for regular *Independent* readers — what happened?'

Erik Neilson swept him aside with one massive hand and clutched his daughter in a bear hug. 'Val! You're all right!'

'I'll be fine if you don't squeeze me to death, Dad. This is Bill Baxter, the other Cisco Kid — he saved me. I need to talk to you in private.

'Sheriff, it was Mueller and he's still free. He's after my father and he'll try again.'

Dutch persisted. 'Mueller? You mean Mr Roach's foreman?'

'Ask the Kid,' she said impatiently. 'He'll tell you about it.'

For a moment the newly arrived river was forgotten as the crowd swarmed around Val Neilson. The Kid and Baxter were cheered and then Dr Paul cleared a path for her.

'Let her through, please. Obviously she's had an ordeal and needs to rest quietly in her own home for a while. You'll hear the full story later.'

Dutch turned quickly to the Kid and Baxter. 'What really happened up there?'

The Kid drawled, 'Mueller used dynamite to blast a natural dam and the river overflowed. It was sure something to see . . . '

As the Kid talked, Neilson urged his daughter into the store and slammed and locked the door after him.

'I've been out of my mind with worry, Val. Even now, I can hardly believe you're back — '

'Mueller,' she interrupted. 'Does the name mean anything to you? Roach's foreman claims you killed his young brother — that you were partners — and he's serious about getting his revenge.'

194

Neilson sat down heavily, his face turning grey, and stared at the floor. He didn't need to speak.

She knelt beside him and held him. After a time, she said fiercely, 'It doesn't matter, Dad. All that's over. You're still the one who's looked after me all these years, and I love you.'

His head came up and he had a wistful expression, but his voice was low when he spoke.

'It's true, Val. I'm so ashamed. I was mad with the lust for gold . . . you can't imagine what it's like when the fever grips you. We slaved, went without food and sleep when we made a strike — and then the fever took over. We both had it. He'd have killed me if I hadn't shot first.'

She gripped his hands tightly, holding him as he lowered his gaze and rambled on.

'Gold fever is the worst sort — it blinds a man to everything else. All I could see was that without him I had all of it. I was rich and nothing else mattered.'

He shuddered. 'I wasn't the only one, Val. A lot of miners turned against their partners when they struck a vein . . . that doesn't excuse me.

'Afterwards, when I came to my senses, I was appalled by what I'd done — but it was too late then. I quit mining and tried to put that part of my life behind me. That was when I came to Oxbow and started this store and married.'

Val said, 'That's in the past. You must think of today. Mueller won't be easily stopped — all he thinks about is revenge. You must speak to the sheriff.' She gave a short laugh. 'Me too — I've my own confession to make.'

Neilson stared blankly. 'You — ?'

★ ★ ★

Back Street was almost deserted when Carl Mueller rode into Oxbow; most people had gone to watch the river rise.

196

He didn't hurry his horse and had his hat tipped forward to shade his face. He'd arrived by a circular route after turning the pack horse loose close to Ferris's land. If Neilson wouldn't come to him he'd use his alternative plan.

He kept going till he reached Griffen's General Store. The building had a lean-to shed behind it and he left his horse there and quietly entered the shop by the rear door, pausing a moment just inside to let his eyes adjust to the shadowed gloom.

There were no customers and the storekeeper had his back to him.

Mueller waited a moment, then spoke in a conversational tone. 'Quiet today.'

Griffen turned and looked steadily at him; he was starting to run to fat and his apron had a grey tinge. He stood among sacks and barrels, his lips pursed as if he were sucking a lemon.

'Here. It's not so quiet on Front Street.'

'Oh?'

'The river's returned, just when we were starting to build new business on Back Street. Now the mayor will get more business from visitors coming to see the riverfront. Have I seen you someplace?'

Mueller said casually, 'It's possible — I used to ride for Mr Roach. What will you do now?'

Griffen shrugged. 'Maybe quit and go somewhere else.'

Mueller made a thin smile and tapped the butt of a revolver. 'There's no need for that. I can take care of Neilson for you.'

Griffen hesitated and glanced around quickly, but they were still alone. 'What would that cost me?'

'Let me stay out of sight till I can get him alone. Feed me and my horse for that time. Then I'll be gone and you'll have your chance at his business.'

Griffen licked his lips. 'You're serious?'

Mueller nodded.

The storekeeper didn't take long to

make up his mind. 'I've a loft you can use . . .'

* * *

Big Joe was not happy. Bounty hunting had its bad moments, but this was a new low. His hand still hurt where the Kid's bullet had smashed it, and he felt naked without a gun.

The only good thing was that he had the weight off his feet. The piebald had the weight and tended to go slow as a result; it stopped to graze too often to suit Joe, and it went down rather than up hills.

The hills appeared barren to Joe except for trees that looked all the same. He'd relied on Bony to find their way across country and now he had little idea where he was; all he knew was that he wanted to be somewhere else.

One-handed, he had difficulty in directing the piebald, which had a mind of its own, even if he'd known which way to go. They drifted along and eventually came to the bed of what once had been a stream; the bottom was still damp and the piebald paused to moisten its lips.

Joe gave it a kick-start and, reluctantly, the pony moved on. Round a bend, a couple of miners stopped panning and eyed him with suspicion. One reached for a gun.

'Keep riding, fella. This is our claim, and you ain't wanted here.'

'Suggest you hurry along,' the second man said. 'We sure ain't got time to bury yuh.'

Joe was tempted to argue — there was a glint of yellow in the riverbed — but he wasn't armed. If he had been . . .

He scowled and rode on. He didn't know it, but his mount was slowly circling to get back to the range it was familiar with.

★ ★ ★

Sheriff Lamming seemed to have taken over his office, the Kid thought. In fact, he appeared to be a back number now. He sat quietly in a corner, enjoying a cigarette and watching Billy and Val hold hands.

The mayor might almost have been somewhere else as he gazed in a distracted way through the open doorway to the crowded riverside; perhaps he expected Mueller to appear out of nowhere.

The sheriff was talking with great earnestness but didn't seem to be getting through.

'Forget what happened years ago, Mr Neilson. You weren't the first to succumb to gold fever and I don't imagine you'll be the last. Anyway, it didn't happen in my county so I'm not interested. Besides, how many votes would I get in Oxbow if I arrested the mayor?'

Neilson showed little interest. His gaze went to Val and then back to the doorway.

Lamming sighed, but went on doggedly.

'Mueller's like a mad dog. He shot down a bounty man without warning and for no reason. He tried to kill Val. He must be stopped before he kills again.'

'It's me he's after,' Neilson muttered.

Lamming nodded. 'True, but he'll kill any bystander who gets in his way — that's what I'm concerned with.'

'I won't let him touch Val,' the mayor said with some of his old vigour.

She brought up her gun. 'He won't get a second chance with me. I intend to shoot first.'

Lamming kept quiet; she'd given the money to him and he'd agreed to return it to the bank without naming her.

'If you see him in time,' the Kid drawled, rolling another cigarette.

'I'll be with you,' Baxter told her. 'Always. And the Kid — we'll see he doesn't get near you.'

The Kid struck a match. 'That's

right, and I doubt if there's a man in Oxbow who won't jump on Mueller if he shows his face here.'

Lamming snorted. 'Fine talk doesn't help us locate him, and we have to find him before we can deal with him. He sure ain't making his whereabouts obvious.'

The Kid drew on his cigarette. 'Reckon he could be anywhere, even here in town right this minute. How many would recognize him?'

The Kid paused, feathering smoke. 'He ain't exactly a regular visitor to Oxbow — and there's a whole parcel of strangers come to see the new waterfront. We need some way to bring him into the open. Any ideas?'

They considered this, but nobody came up with an idea. In the pause, a man stepped through the doorway and said, 'You're the one I'm looking for, Sheriff.'

It was Roach, owner of the Big R.

16

Trouble with Water

'You've found me,' Lamming said. 'What is it?'

The rancher didn't answer immediately. He was staring at Val Neilson in surprise. 'You're back? I heard you were — '

She was not amused. 'Yes, I'm still alive, no thanks to your foreman.'

'Mueller?' Roach rubbed the side of his nose, and frowned. 'Are you telling me he had something to do with whatever happened?'

'Yes, Mr Roach. It was your foreman who abducted me — with the intention of killing me.'

'I hope you don't think I had anything to do with that? As you know I had hoped . . . ' The Big R rancher looked at Baxter, who was holding her hand possessively. 'Seems you might be throwing away your best chance.'

'It was Bill Baxter who saved me — where were you?'

'More important, d'yuh know where Mueller is now?' the Kid cut in. 'I seem to recall you bought a case of dynamite, Mr Roach.'

'That's not a crime . . . and I'd like to know where he is too.'

'Figure you gave it to Mueller — to blast a natural dam so the river would change course.'

Roach began to look hunted. His face turned red and he blustered.

'That's why I'm here! My land has lost its normal flow of water, and Ferris and the other small fry are denying my cattle access to the new course of the river. They claim it's their water on their land! I want you, Sheriff, to tell them they've got to let my herd drink wherever the water is and enforce the law.'

The Kid laughed as if it were a good joke. 'Maybe you reckoned to get all the water flowing on to your land? If the idea worked the opposite way, too bad!'

'Sheriff, I want the law with me when I drive my cattle to water. All my men will be armed and ready to shoot if — '

Lamming shook his head. 'No, Mr Roach, it won't do. The days when a cattle baron could ride roughshod over everyone else have gone. You've over-reached yourself this time.'

The boss of Big R shook with fury. 'Then stay out of it — I'll deal with these two-bit outfits my way!'

He wheeled around and stormed out of the marshal's office.

Lamming sighed. 'Guess I'll need to ride. I can't let him start a range war.' He nodded to the Kid and Baxter. 'I'll leave you two to deal with Mueller.'

Dutch Holland was happy as he set his largest type. He hummed a cheerful tune and might have danced a jig if he'd been able to set type at the same time. This was the sort of copy he enjoyed. A headline read:

'Publicity,' he chuckled. 'I'll give you publicity you'll never forget!'

His pudgy fingers moved deftly, selecting and placing type for a special edition of the *Independent* quicker than Val's eyes could follow.

It has come to our attention that the marshal of Prospect is trying to cut in on the Cisco Kid's courting of Miss Neilson —

She sniffed. 'Not true — I was the one doing the courting!'

'Our readers prefer it this way,' Dutch said. 'It's the natural order.'

And while the people of Oxbow are grateful to Mr Baxter for his part in rescuing the mayor's daughter, now we say, 'Go home, Bill Baxter!'

'That's not what I say,' Val murmured rebelliously.

*The Kid has issued his challenge
— if you stay, he will be forced to
kill you — so stop interfering in
our big romance and return to
Prospect.*

'It's my big romance!'
Dutch ignored her; he was busy
estimating the number of visitors to
Oxbow's waterfront, ready to run off
extra copies of his paper.

★　★　★

Baxter said, 'It's too risky. I'm not
chancing Val getting hurt.'
The two Kids and Val were alone in
the hotel dining-room chewing on
generous portions of steak and dump-
lings smothered in thick gravy.
She flared up immediately. 'I'll take
any risk to protect my dad. If you think
you're going to hide me away somewhere, like a china cup, you can forget
it. I've something to settle with Mueller
myself!'

The Cisco Kid stabbed at a piece of meat with his knife. This had been his idea.

'Mueller is a dangerous man, no argument, so we all take some risk. That's unavoidable. There's been no sighting of him, but this way we've a chance to lure him out from wherever he's hiding. Only then will we get a clear shot at him.'

'I don't want him taking a shot at Val,' Baxter said doggedly.

'Oh, of course not,' she snapped. 'I wonder you don't want to wrap me up in cotton wool!'

The Kid smiled. 'We have to spot him and shoot first. Dutch is co-operating, so everyone in town knows to expect a show-down on Front Street at a set time — and only a few will know we're faking it. Most people will flock to watch and that's his chance; all eyes will be on the two of us. Mueller will come out of hiding — and then we'll nail him.'

'If he doesn't nail us first,' Baxter said gloomily.

* * *

Sheriff Lamming left his buggy at the livery stable, slung a saddle over the back of his horse and rode out of Oxbow, following the new course of the river. He was in no doubt of the seriousness of the situation; Roach was one of the old breed of rancher who reckoned they could take anything they wanted by force of arms.

It had worked in the past, and he couldn't see that his time was over and the law ruled now. Lamming knew, too, that more trouble arose from water rights than any other factor on a cattle range. Roach would be in a hurry to rejoin his men.

And with an election coming up, the sheriff was in no mood to put up with troublemakers. But still he didn't force the pace; he wanted to keep his mount fresh for what lay ahead. Further along, he saw Ferris with a bunch of small ranchers and reined back to study them.

210

These were the men trying to compete with the Big R. They looked happy as they watched their cattle drink at the new river. They carried rifles and looked ready and determined; young family men, old cowhands, each had a stake in the land.

Ferris pushed back his weathered Stetson as he came up. 'Glad to see you, Sheriff. I figure Roach will be along shortly with his crew, and we need the law on our side. This is our land and that makes this our water.'

Lamming nodded curtly. 'Maybe. Personally, I don't give a damn whose land it is or where the water runs. I'm telling you I'm here to stop any trouble.'

'You'll tell Roach that, I hope?'

'I'll tell him. I won't stand for a range war in my county.'

'If he starts it,' Ferris said grimly, 'we'll meet lead with lead.'

'Don't be a fool. Big R outnumber you and cattle need water. You know that as well as I do or Roach does.'

Another rancher chimed in. 'We've heard the tale, how Roach sent his hired gun with dynamite to change the course of the river so he'd get all the water.'

'I'm not interested,' Lamming said.

'Then you'd better get interested.' Ferris pointed at a distant dust cloud.

'That's a herd coming — and Roach and his outfit will be aiming to shoot first. Now let's see the law in action.'

Lamming squinted in sunlight. Dust rose in great billows and hoofs drummed. Flanking the herd came riders holding rifles as the cows headed directly for the river.

'You men stay here and keep out of this,' he told Ferris. 'I'll arrest the first man to use a gun.'

He turned his back on the bunched ranchers and rode towards the oncoming herd. He had to get between the two groups and stay there; that was his one chance to prevent open warfare.

He rubbed dust from his badge and

polished it so it shone in the sun and started towards Roach and his riders. He had almost reached them when he heard the first gunshot.

17

Riverfront Shoot-Out

It was gloomy in the loft. Mueller had to hold the newspaper slantwise and close to a crack to get enough light to read by.

It appeared that Val Neilson was being fought over by the two Cisco Kids, like a bone by two dogs . . . a duel at noon on the waterfront.

Mueller grunted. He already knew, from Griffen, that she'd survived.

A smell of ham drifted up from below; and Mueller was already fed up with an exclusive diet of ham.

Griffen, standing on bare wooden steps leading up to the loft, regarded him slyly. 'Figured this was maybe a chance for yuh. Folk'll be watching them two, betting on one or the other.'

Mueller's mind raced. 'It's today.

What's the time now?'

'Coming up to the hour — it wants a few minutes yet, even if they get the timing right.'

Mueller considered the idea. There'd be a crowd but all eyes would be on the two Kids. He made up his mind and picked up his rifle. He jammed the barrel into a crack in the plank roof, forcing an opening.

'Hi,' Griffen said, alarmed. 'What yuh doing that for?'

When he'd made a big enough opening, Mueller said, 'Give me a boost.'

Still grumbling, Griffen obeyed. Mueller went up, thrust his rifle on to the roof and climbed after it.

He studied the rooftops spread out before him, flat and slanting, adobe and sod; the roof of the store sloped towards that of a building on Front Street. There was an empty yard between but he could jump that.

He felt exhilarated; nobody would expect him to come over the roofs and shoot from above so he'd have the element of surprise. He took his time, moving cautiously, calculated the width of the gap, and jumped. He landed full length, dropping forward, scrambled upright and moved immediately towards the other side of the building.

He was looking down on Front Street, the near side crowded with excited spectators, the far side aswirl with water. He saw the two Kids one at each end of the street. They stood, waiting. He scanned the crowd.

Where was Neilson? Or Val? She, at least, must be watching. Get her and Neilson would come running. He checked his rifle and raised it, waiting, licking his lips in anticipation.

He saw the referee drop a handkerchief and the Kids began a slow walk towards each other.

This was his day, his moment. He remembered Peter as his finger curled about the trigger.

★ ★ ★

Young Oliver didn't intend to put a foot wrong; he was fed up being considered a greenhorn by the men of the Big R.

He was riding flank as they moved the herd slowly across the range, pleased that he wasn't eating dust. The boss was up front, leading, and another rider covered the opposite flank, the rest of the crew came along behind.

The foreman wasn't with them; and strange rumours circulated among the hands to account for his absence.

The cows began to smell water and quickened their step. Somewhere ahead the smalltime ranchers would be gathered to repulse them. Maybe there'd be shooting, and Oliver was excited, determined to get everything right this time.

Then, way over to his right he glimpsed a lone rider drifting towards the herd. He stared, not recognizing the horseman. Could it be one of Ferris's bunch pulling a sneak attack? Oliver drew his rifle from its scabbard.

Suddenly he recognized the horse, a piebald. The Big R's wanderer, with a stranger in the saddle. A horse-thief, for sure. He veered towards the piebald, pleased; if he could recapture one of the boss's horses . . .

The rider noticed him and changed direction. Oliver pushed his horse to a gallop, brought up his gun and fired. And again. And a third time.

The piebald bolted, shaking its rider loose; he clung to the mane with one hand for brief seconds, then hit the ground and stayed unmoving while the wanderer headed for the horizon.

Too late Oliver realized it wasn't only the horse he'd scared. The cattle were bolting too. His shots had sparked off a stampede.

Groaning his dismay, he turned his mount and galloped after the herd, trying to catch up and help turn the leaders. But he was too far behind.

The cows were tightly bunched and running faster and faster, making for the river.

★ ★ ★

Bill Baxter — Val insisted he no longer used the diminutive — walked stiff-legged along Front Street between a crowd of spectators and the river towards the Cisco Kid.

Bluff, he thought, recalling the Kid's words, and acutely aware he wouldn't stand a chance if this was for real. He felt shaky, legs trembling, even though there was no risk the Kid would hit him. His stomach wasn't convinced.

He tried to focus on faces, waiting for Mueller's to show. He imagined Val's; she was with her father, watching from inside the store.

He heard excited voices laying odds against him, and smiled faintly. One step closer to the Kid, hand hovering over the butt of his Colt revolver; and another, each step slow and deliberate.

How many times had Hank Judson walked down Main Street to face a gunman dressed in black? And won? But never quite like this . . .

He saw the Kid's gaze swivelling all the time, keen and alert, searching: but still there was no sign of Roach's foreman. Was he even in Oxbow?

The gap was steadily closing, spectators holding their breath; another step. As far as the crowd knew, one of the duellists was about to die. Another step. He could smell the river.

They had to go through with it, Baxter thought; they were too close to duck out now.

He went for his gun and the Cisco Kid, in one fluid movement, drew and squeezed the trigger while he was still bringing his revolver up.

Baxter felt the wind as the bullet passed close to his head; he managed a convincing stagger and crumpled to the ground. That part took no effort. He heard a long drawn-out sigh from the crowd. Now he had to wait, gun in hand, eyes open watching. He was aware of the Kid, alert, looking everywhere.

Then Val Neilson came running out

of the store, towards him, crying 'Bill!'

And, suddenly, the Kid's head jerked upwards . . .

★   ★   ★

'Damn fool,' Lamming muttered, when two more shots followed in quick succession. He knew, as well as any range rider, that cattle spook easily. And these were beginning to run.

The drumming of hoofs changed to a noise like thunder as they gathered speed, the rear animals pressing against those in front and driving them forward.

The sheriff's horse didn't wait for an order; it gave a snort, jerked around and bolted. Lamming clung to the saddlehorn and leaned forward as his hat was carried away.

He glanced back once; the leading steers had their horns lowered as they ran for the river. He glimpsed Roach, white-faced, at their head, spurring his mount. Then the first cows caught up with him, a horn gored and brought down his horse. He was engulfed. The Big R rancher disappeared in a sea of clashing horns and hoofs.

Lamming let his horse have its head. In a cold sweat he knew he didn't have time to turn aside. Ahead he saw Ferris and his fellow ranchers scatter like tumbleweed before a storm.

He had to reach the river first and swim it; no one caught in that mad charge was going to survive. The stampede would peter out when the leaders reached water and began to drink.

His horse was frothing at the mouth, galloping in panic to avoid certain death. Close behind, sharp horns rattled as they clashed. The sheriff clung on desperately as his horse plunged into water.

★ ★ ★

Erik Neilson ran from his store, swearing, when he saw his daughter dart towards Baxter. She knew the duel was faked so why was she showing herself? He had to stop her.

He was still cursing, calling her name when he saw the Kid bring up his gun and heard him shout, 'Mueller! On the roof!'

He had almost reached her when he heard a single shot and felt savage pain in his back. He fell forward, gasping for breath . . . glimpsed Val's white face.

'*Dad!*'

His mouth filled with blood and he couldn't tell her he was sorry for the past, that he loved her . . .

Baxter scrambled to his feet, too late. The Kid had a clear view of the figure on the roof and kept triggering shots till his revolver was empty.

The slugs turned Mueller around when they hit him and he stumbled, dropping his rifle. He toppled from his high perch and scattered the crowd as he fell to the riverfront.

For a moment there was silence; both duellists were alive, so whose was this unexpected corpse?

Baxter walked unsteadily towards Val, cradling her father's head with tears streaming down her face; he didn't need to look closely to know that Neilson was beyond medical aid.

He raised her up and held her; she was shaking violently and sticky with blood. As she clung to him, the Cisco Kid brought his mare from the livery and rode quietly away.

★　★　★

Some months later, after Colonel Gus Whitney had dispensed with his services, Baxter married Val and settled down to run Neilson's store. Eventually, the news got through: neither Prospect nor Oxbow would be state capital — but Sheriff Lamming had been nominated state governor.

By then, the people of Oxbow were no longer interested. Miners were working the riverbed exposed when Carl Mueller blasted a natural dam, and bringing in enough gold to turn Oxbow into a boom town.

Bill Baxter was run off his feet and Val was expecting their first-born when he came across an old copy of *Hank Judson — Fighting Marshal*; and it seemed to him as he glanced through it that the adventures of his once-favourite hero would never seem quite the same again.